Richard Hurd, Horace, William Mason

Q. Horatii Flacci Epistolae ad Pisones, et Augustum

Volume 2

Richard Hurd, Horace, William Mason

Q. Horatii Flacci Epistolae ad Pisones, et Augustum
Volume 2

ISBN/EAN: 9783337399306

Printed in Europe, USA, Canada, Australia, Japan

Cover: Foto ©Andreas Hilbeck / pixelio.de

Q. HORATII FLACCI
EPISTOLAE
AD
PISONES,
ET
AUGUSTUM:

WITH AN ENGLISH
COMMENTARY AND NOTES:
TO WHICH ARE ADDED
CRITICAL DISSERTATIONS.

BY THE
REVEREND MR. HURD.

THE FIFTH EDITION,
CORRECTED AND ENLARGED.

VOL. II.

LONDON,
PRINTED BY W. BOWYER AND J. NICHOLS:
FOR T. CADELL, IN THE STRAND; AND
J. WOODYER, AT CAMBRIDGE.
MDCCLXXVI.

TO THE REVEREND

MR. WARBURTON.

REVEREND SIR,

GIVE me leave to preſent to you the following Eſſay on the *Epiſtle to Auguſtus*; which, whatever other merit it may want, is ſecure of this, that it hath been planned upon the beſt model. For I know not what ſhould hinder me from declaring to you in this public manner, that it was the early pleaſure I received from what you had written of this ſort, which *firſt* engaged me in the province of criticiſm. And, if I have taken upon me to illuſtrate *another* of the fineſt pieces of antiquity after the *ſame method*, it is becauſe I find myſelf encouraged to do ſo by higher conſiderations, than even the Authority of your example.

CRITICISM, conſidered in its antient and nobleſt office of doing juſtice to the merits of great writers, more eſpecially in works of poetry and invention, demands, to its perfect execution, theſe two qualities: *a philoſophic ſpirit*, capable of penetrating the fundamental reaſons of excellence in every different ſpecies of compoſition; and *a ſtrong imagination*, the parent of what we call *true taſte*, enabling the critic to feel the full force of his author's excellence himſelf, and to impreſs a lively ſenſe of it upon others. Each of theſe abilities is neceſſary. For by means of philoſophy, criticiſm, which were otherwiſe a vague and ſuperficial thing,

acquires

acquires the ſoundneſs and ſolidity of ſcience. And from the *power of fancy*, it derives that light and energy and ſpirit, which are wanting to provoke the public emulation and carry the general concluſions of reaſon into practice.

Of theſe talents (to regard them in their ſeparate ſtate) that of a *ſtrong imagination*, as being the commoner of the two, one would naturally ſuppoſe ſhould be the firſt to exert itſelf in the ſervice of criticiſm. And thus it ſeems, in fact, to have happened. For there were very early in Greece a ſort of men, who, under the name of RHAPSODISTS, made it their buſineſs to illuſtrate the beauties of their favourite writers. Though their art, indeed, was very ſimple; for it conſiſted only in *acting* the fineſt paſſages of their works, and in *repeating* them, with a rapturous kind of vehemence, to an ecſtatic auditory. Whence it appears, that criticiſm, as being yet in its infancy, was wholly turned to *admiration*; a paſſion which true *judgment* as little indulges in the ſchools of *Art*, as ſound philoſophy, in thoſe of *Nature*. Accordingly theſe enraptured declaimers, though they travelled down to the politer ages, could not ſubſiſt in them. The fine ridicule of Plato, in one of his Dialogues [a], and the growing taſte for juſt thinking, ſeem perfectly to have diſcredited this folly. And it was preſently ſeen and acknowledged even by the Rhapſodiſt himſelf, that, how *divinely* ſoever he might feel himſelf affected by the magnetic virtue of the muſe, yet, as he could give no intelligible account of its ſubtle operations, he was aſſuredly no *Artiſt*; ΘΕΙΟΝ εἶναι καὶ μὴ ΤΕΧΝΙΚΟΝ ἐπαινέτην.

[a] ΊΩΝ.

From

From this time they, who took upon themſelves the office of commenting and recommending the great-writers of Greece, diſcharged it in a very different manner. Their reſearches grew ſevere, inquiſitive, and rational. And no wonder; for the perſon, who now took the lead in theſe ſtudies, and ſet the faſhion of them, was a *philoſopher*, and, which was happy for the advancement of this art, the juſteſt philoſopher of antiquity. Hence *ſcientific* or ſpeculative criticiſm attained to perfection, at once; and appeared in all that ſeverity of reaſon and accuracy of method, which Ariſtotle himſelf could beſtow upon it.

But now this might almoſt ſeem as violent an extreme as the other. For though to *underſtand* be better than to *admire*, yet the generality of readers *cannot*, or *will not*, underſtand, where there is *nothing* for them to admire.

So that *reaſon*, for her own ſake, is obliged to borrow ſomething of the dreſs, and to mimic the airs, of *fancy*: And Ariſtotle's *reaſon* was too proud to ſubmit to this management.

Hence, the critical plan, which the Stagyrite had formed with ſuch rigour of ſcience, however it might ſatisfy the curious ſpeculatiſt, wanted to be *relieved* and ſet off to the common eye by the heightenings of eloquence. This, I obſerved, was the eaſier taſk of the two; and yet it was very long before it was *ſucceſsfully* attempted. Amongſt other reaſons of this delay, the principal, as you obſerve, might be the fall of the public freedom of Greece, which ſoon after followed. For then, inſtead of the free and manly efforts of genius, which alone could accompliſh ſuch a reformation, the trifling ſpirit of the times declined into mere verbal amuſements. " Whence, as you ſay, ſo

" great

"great a cloud of ſcholiaſts and gram-
"marians ſo ſoon overſpread the
"learning of Greece, when once that
"famous community had loſt its
"liberty [b]."

And what Greece was thus unable, of a long time, to furniſh, we ſhall in vain ſeek in another great community, which ſoon after flouriſhed in all liberal ſtudies. The genius of Rome was bold and elevated enough for this taſk. But Criticiſm of any kind was little cultivated, never profeſſed as an *art*, by this people. The ſpecimens we have of their ability in this way (of which the moſt elegant, beyond diſpute, are the two epiſtles to *Auguſtus* and the *Piſos*) are ſlight occaſional attempts; made in the negligence of common ſenſe, and adapted to the peculiar exigencies of their own taſte and learning: and not by any

[b] Pope's Works, vol. v. p. 244. 8vo.

means

means the regular productions of *art*, professedly bending itself to this work, and ambitious to give the last finishing to the critical system.

For so great an effort as this, we are to look back to the confines of Greece. And there at length, and even from beneath the depression of slavery (but with a spirit that might have done honour to its age of greatest liberty), a CRITIC arose, singularly qualified for so generous an undertaking. His profession, which was that of a *rhetorical sophist*, required him to be fully instructed in the graces and embellishments of eloquence; and these, the vigour of his genius enabled him to comprehend in their utmost force and beauty. In a word, LONGINUS was the person, whom, of all the critics of antiquity, nature seems to have formed with the proper talents to give the last honour to his profeſſion, and penetrate the very ſoul of fine writing.

Yet ſo bounded is human *wit*, and with ſuch difficulty is human *art* compleated, that even here the advantage, which had been ſo fortunately gained on the one hand, was, in great meaſure, loſt and forfeited on the other. He had ſoftened indeed the ſeverity of Ariſtotle's plan; but, in doing this, had gone back again too far into the manner of the admiring Rhapſodiſt. In ſhort, with the brighteſt views of nature and true beauty, which the fineſt imagination could afford to the beſt critic, he now wanted, in a good degree, that preciſion, and depth of thought, which had ſo eminently diſtinguiſhed his predeceſſor. For, as Plotinus long ago obſerved of him, *though he had approved himſelf a maſter of polite literature, he was* NO *Philoſopher*; ΦΙΛΟΛΟΓΟΣ ΜΕΝ, ΦΙΛΟΣΟΦΟΣ ΔΕ ΟΥΔΑΜΩΣ.

Thus

Thus the art had been ſhifting reciprocally into two extremes. And in one or other of theſe extremes, it was likely to continue. For the fame and eminent ability of their great founders had made them conſidered as *models*, in their different ways, of perfect criticiſm. Only it was eaſy to foreſee which of them the humour of ſucceeding times would be moſt diſpoſed to emulate. The catching enthuſiaſm and picturesque fancy of the *one* would be ſure to prevail over the coolneſs and auſterity of the *other*. Accordingly in the laſt and preſent century, when now the diligence of learned men had, by reſtoring the purity, opened an eaſy way to the ſtudy, of the old claſſics, a numberleſs tribe of commentators have attempted, after the manner of Longinus, to *flouriſh* on the excellencies of their compoſition. And ſome of them, indeed, ſucceeded ſo well in this method,

thod, that one is not to wonder it soon became the popular and only authorized form of what was reputed *just Criticism*. Yet, as nothing but superior genius could make it tolerable even in the best of these, it was to be expected (what experience hath now fully shewn), that it would at length, and in ordinary hands, degenerate into the most unmeaning, frivolous, and disgustful jargon, that ever discredited polite letters.

This, Sir, was the state in which you received *modern Criticism*: a state, which could only shew you, that, of the two models, antiquity had furnished to our use, we had learned, by an awkward imitation of it, to abuse the *worst*. But it did not content your zeal for the service of letters barely to remedy this *abuse*. It was not enough, in your enlarged view of things, to restore either of these models to its antient ſplendour. They were both to be revived; or rather a new original plan of criticiſm was to be ſtruck out, which ſhould unite the virtues of each of them. The experiment was made on the TWO greateſt of our own poets; and, by reflecting all the lights of the imagination on the ſevereſt reaſon, every thing was effected, which the warmeſt admirer of antient art could promiſe to himſelf from ſuch an union. But you went farther. By joining to theſe powers a perfect inſight into human nature, and ſo ennobling the exerciſe of *literary*, by the addition of the juſteſt moral, cenſure, you have now, at length, advanced CRITICISM to its full glory.

Not but, conſidering the inveterate foible of mankind, which the poet ſo juſtly ſatirizes in the following work, I mean that, which diſpoſes them to malign and depreciate all the efforts of wit and virtue, —niſi

— nisi quae terris semota suisque
Temporibus defuncta videt —

Considering, I say, this temper of mankind, you may sooner, perhaps, expect the censures of the dull and envious of all denominations, than the candid applause of the public, even for this service.

I apprehend this consequence the rather, because criticism, though it be *the last fruit of literary experience*, is more exposed to the cavils of ignorance and vanity, than, perhaps, any other species of learned application: all men being forward to judge, and few men giving themselves leave to doubt of their being able to judge, of the merits of well-known and popular writers.

Nor is this all: When writers of a certain rank condescend to this work of criticism, the innovation excites a very

very natural ferment in the *men of the profession*.

Their JEALOUSY is alarmed, as if there was a design to strip them of the only honour they can reasonably pretend to, that of sitting in judgment on the *inventions* of their betters. But to JUDGE, as well as to INVENT, is thought a violent encroachment in the republic of Letters; not unlike the ambition of the Roman emperors, who would be consuls, and censors too, that is, would have the privilege of excluding from the senate, as well as of presiding in it.

But if jealousy were out of the case, their MALIGNITY would be much inflamed by this intrusion. For who can bear to see his own weak endeavours, in any art, disgraced by a consummate model?

Besides, to say the truth, the conceptions of such writers, as I before

spoke

ſpoke of, lie ſo remote from vulgar apprehenſion, that, without either *jealouſy* or *malignity*, DULLNESS itſelf will be ſure to create them many peeviſh detractors. For an ordinary critic can ſcarce help finding fault with what he does not underſtand, or being angry where he has no ideas.

On all theſe accounts, it may poſſibly happen, as I ſaid, that your critical labours will draw upon you much popular reſentment and invective.

But if ſuch ſhould be the *preſent* effect of your endeavours to cultivate and complete this elegant part of literature; you, who know the temper of the learned world, and, by your eminent merits, have ſo oft provoked its injuſtice, will not be diſturbed or ſurprized at it: much leſs ſhould it diſcourage thoſe who are diſpoſed to do you more right, from celebrating, and, as they find themſelves able, from copying your example;

For USE will father what's begot by SENSE,

as well in this, as in other inſtances.

YOU SEE, Sir, what there is of encomium in the turn of this Letter, was intended not ſo much for your ſake, as my own. Had my purpoſe been any other, I muſt have choſen very ill among the various parts of your character to take *this* for the ſubject of an addreſs to you. For, after all I have ſaid and think of your critical abilities, it might ſeem almoſt as ſtrange in a panegyriſt on Mr. Warburton to tell of his admirable criticiſms on POPE and SHAKESPEARE, as it would be in him, who ſhould deſign an encomium on Socrates, to inſiſt on his excellent ſculp-

ture

ture of MERCURY and the GRACES. Yet there is a time, when it may be allowed to lay a ſtreſs on the amuſements of ſuch men. It is, when an adventurer in either *art* would do an honour to his profeſſion.

I am,

with the trueſt eſteem,

Reverend Sir,

Your moſt obedient

and moſt humble ſervant,

CAMBRIDGE,
March 29, 1753.

R. HURD.

Q. HORATII FLACCI

EPISTOLA AD AUGUSTUM.

CUM tot ſuſtineas et tanta negotia ſolus,
Res Italas armis tuteris, moribus ornes,
Legibus emendes; in publica commoda peccem,
Si longo ſermone morer tua tempora, Caeſar.

COMMENTARY.

EPISTOLA AD AUGUSTUM.] In conducting this work, which is *an apology for the poets of his own time*, the method of the writer is no other, than that which plain ſenſe, and the ſubject itſelf, required of him. For, as the main diſlike to the Auguſtan poets had ariſen from an *exceſſive reverence* paid to their elder brethren, the *firſt* part of the epiſtle [from line 1 to 118] is very naturally laid out in the ridicule and confutation of ſo abſurd a prejudice. And having, by this preparation, obtained a candid hearing for his defence, he then proceeds [in what follows, to the *end*] to vindicate their real *merits*; ſetting in view the excellencies of the *Latin poetry*, as cultivated by the great modern maſters; and throwing the blame of their ill ſucceſs, and of the contempt in which they had lain, not ſo much on themſelves, or their *profeſſion* (the dignity of *which*, in particular, he inſiſts highly upon, and aſſerts with ſpirit) as on the vicious

Romulus, et Liber pater, et cum Castore Pollux,
Post ingentia fata, Deorum in templa recepti,
Dum terras hominumque colunt genus, aspera bella
Conponunt, agros adsignant, oppida condunt;
Ploravere suis non respondere favorem
Speratum meritis. diram qui contudit Hydram,
Notaque fatali portenta labore subegit,
Comperit invidiam supremo fine domari.

COMMENTARY.

taste of the age, and certain unfavouring circumstances, which had accidentally concurred to dishonour *both*.

This idea of the *general* plan being comprehended, the reader will find it no difficulty to perceive the order and arrangement of *particular* parts, which the natural transition of the poet's thought insensibly drew along with it.

5—118. ROMULUS, ET LIBER PATER, &c.] The subject commences from line 5, where, by a contrivance of great beauty, a pertinent *illustration* of the poet's argument becomes an offering of the happiest *address* to the emperor. Its *double* purpose may be seen thus. His primary intention was to take off the force of prejudice against *modern* poets, arising from the superior veneration of the *antients*. To this end the first thing wanting was to demonstrate by some striking instance, that it was, indeed, nothing but *prejudice*; which he does effectually in taking that instance from the *heroic*, that is, the most revered, ages. For if such, whose acknowledged virtues and eminent services

Urit enim fulgore suo, qui praegravat artis
Infra se positas: extinctus amabitur idem.
Praesenti tibi maturos largimur honores,
Jurandasque tuum per numen ponimus aras,
Nil oriturum alias, nil ortum tale fatentes.
Sed tuus hoc populus sapiens et justus in uno,
Te nostris ducibus, te Graiis anteferendo,
Cetera nequaquam simili ratione modoque

COMMENTARY.

services had raised them to the rank of *heroes*, that is, in the pagan conception of things, to the honours of *divinity*, could not secure their fame, in their own times, against the malevolence of slander, what wonder that the race of wits, whose obscurer merit is less likely to dazzle the public eye, and yet, by a peculiar fatality, is more apt to awaken its jealousy, should find themselves oppressed by its rudest censure? In the *former* case, the honours, which equal posterity paid to excelling worth, declare all *such* censure to have been the calumny of malice only. What reason then to conclude, it had any other original in the *latter*? This is the poet's *argument*.

But now, of these worthies themselves, whom the justice of grateful posterity had snatched out of the hands of detraction, there were some, it seems, whose illustrious services the virtue, or vain-glory of the emperor, most affected to emulate; and these, therefore, the poet, by an ingenious flattery, selects for examples to his general *observation*,

Romulus, et Liber pater, et cum Castore Pollux
Post ingentia facta, &c.

 Farther,

Aeſtimat; et, niſi quae terris ſemota ſuiſque
Temporibus defuncta videt, faſtidit et odit:
Sic fautor veterum, ut Tabulas peccare vetantis,
Quas bis quinque viri ſanxerunt, Foedera regum
Vel Gabiis vel cum rigidis aequata Sabinis,
Pontificum libros, annoſa volumina Vatum,

COMMENTARY.

Further, as the good fortune of Auguſtus, though adorned with the *ſame* enviable qualities, had exempted *him* from the injuries which had conſtantly befallen *thoſe admired characters*, this peculiar circumſtance in the hiſtory of his prince affords him the happieſt occaſion, flattery could deſire, of paying diſtinguiſhed honours to his glory.

Praeſenti tibi maturos largimur honores.

And this conſtitutes the fine *addreſs and compliment of his application.*

But this juſtice, which Auguſtus had exacted, as it were, by the very authority of his virtue, from his applauding people, was but ill diſcharged in other inſtances.

Sed tuus hoc populus ſapiens et juſtus in uno,
Te noſtris ducibus, te Graiis anteferendo,
Cetera nequaquam ſimili ratione modoque
Aeſtimat, &c.

And thus the very *exception* to the general rule, which forms the encomium, leads him with advantage into his *argument*; which was to obſerve and expoſe "the "malignant influence of prepoſſeſſion, in obſtructing "the proper glories of living merit." So that, as good ſenſe demands in every reaſonable panegyric, the praiſe reſults from the nature and foundation of the

Dictitet Albano Musas in monte locutas.
Si, quia Graiorum sunt antiquissima quaeque
Scripta vel optima, Romani pensantur eadem
Scriptores trutina; non est quod multa loquamur:
Nil intra est olea, nil extra est in nuce duri:
Venimus ad summum fortunae: pinginius, atque

COMMENTARY.

the subject-matter, and is not violently and reluctantly dragged into it.

His general charge against his countrymen, "of "their bigoted attachment to those, dignified by the "name of *antients*, in prejudice to the just deserts of "the moderns," being thus delivered; and the folly of such conduct, with some agreeable exaggeration, exposed; he sets himself, with a happy mixture of irony and argument, as well becomes the genius and character of the *epistle*, to confute the pretences, and overturn the very *foundations*, on which it rested.

One main support of their folly was taken from an allowed fact, viz. "That the oldest *Greek* writers "were incontestably superior to the modern ones." From whence they inferred, that it was but according to nature and the course of experience, to give the like preference to the oldest *Roman* masters.

His confutation of this sophism consists of two parts. *First*, [from line 28 to 32,] he insists on the *evident* absurdity of the opinion he is confuting. There was no reasoning with persons capable of such *extravagant positions*. But, *secondly*, the pretended fact itself, with regard to the Greek learning, was *grossly misunderstood, or perversely applied*. For [from line 32 to 34] it was not true, nor could it be admitted, that the

Psallimus, et luctamur Achivis doctius unctis.
Si meliora dies, ut vina, poemata reddit;
Scire velim, chartis pretium quotus arrogat annus,
Scriptor ab hinc annos centum qui decidit, inter
Perfectos veteresque referri debet, an inter
Vilis atque novos? excludat jurgia finis.
Est vetus atque probus centum qui perficit annos.
Quid? qui deperiit minor uno mense vel anno,

COMMENTARY.

very *oldest* of the *Greek* writers were the best, but those only, which were old, in comparison of the mere modern Greeks. The so much applauded models of Grecian antiquity were themselves *modern*, in respect of the still *older* and ruder essays of their first writers. It was long discipline and cultivation, the same which had given the Greek *artists* in the Augustan reign a superiority over the Roman, that by degrees established the good taste, and fixed the authority, of the Greek *poets*; from which point it was natural, and even necessary for succeeding, *i. e.* the modern, Greeks to decline. But no consequence lay from hence to the advantage of the Latin poets, in question; who were wholly unfurnished with any previous study of the arts of verse; and whose works could only be compared with the very *oldest*, that is, the rude, foregotten essays of the Greek poetry. So that the fine sense, so closely shut up in this concise couplet, comes out thus: "The modern Greek masters of the *fine arts* "are confessedly superior to the modern Roman. "The reason is, they have practised them longer, "and with more diligence. Just so, the modern

"Roman

Inter quos referendus erit? veteresne poetas,
An quos et praesens et postera respuat aetas?
Iste quidem veteres inter ponetur honeste,
Qui vel mense brevi, vel toto est junior anno.
Utor permisso, caudaeque pilos ut equinae
Paullatim vello; et demo unum, demo et item unum;
Dum cadat elusus ratione ruentis acervi,
Qui redit in fastos, et virtutem aestimat annis.

COMMENTARY.

"Roman writers must needs have the advantage of "their *old* ones: who had no knowledge of writing, "as an *art*, or, if they had, took but small care to put "it in practice."

Further, this plea of antiquity is as uncertain in its *application*, as it was destitute of all truth and reason in its original *foundation*. For if age only must bear away the palm, what way is there of determining, which writers are *modern*, and which *ancient*? The impossibility of fixing this to the satisfaction of an objector, which is pursued [to line 50] with much agreeable raillery, makes it evident, that the circumstance of antiquity is absolutely nothing; and that, in *estimating the merit* of writers, the real, intrinsic excellence of their writings *themselves* is alone to be regarded.

Thus far the poet's intent was to combat the *general* prejudice of the critic,

Qui redit in fastos, et virtutem aestimat annis.

Taking the fact for granted "of his strong prepos-"session for antiquity, *as such*" he would discredit,

Miraturque nihil, niſi quod Libitina ſacravit.
Ennius et ſapiens, et fortis, et alter Homerus,
Ut critici dicunt, leviter curare videtur
Quo promiſſa cadant, et ſomnia Pythagorea.
Naevius in manibus non eſt, et mentibus haeret
Pene recens? adeo ſanctum eſt vetus omne poema.
Ambigitur quotiens, uter utro ſit prior; aufert
Pacuvius docti famam ſenis, Accius alti:
Dicitur Afranî toga conveniſſe Menandro:
Plautus ad exemplar Siculi properare Epicharmi:

COMMENTARY.

both by raillery and argument, ſo abſurd a conduct. What he gains by this diſpoſition, is to come to the *particulars* of his charge with more advantage. For the popular contempt of modern compoſition, ſheltering itſelf under a ſhew of learned admiration of the *antients*, whoſe age and reputation had made them truly venerable, and whoſe genuine merits, in the main, could not be diſputed, a direct attack upon their fame, at ſetting out, without any ſoftening, had diſguſted the moſt *moderate*; whereas this prefatory appeal to common ſenſe, under the cover of general criticiſm, would even diſpoſe bigotry itſelf to afford the poet a candid hearing. His accuſation then of the public taſte comes in here very pertinently; and is delivered, with addreſs [from line 50 to 63] in a particular detail of the judgments paſſed upon the moſt celebrated of the old Roman poets, by the generality of the modern critics; where, to win upon their prejudices ſtill further by his generoſity and good faith,

he

Vincere Caecilius gravitate, Terentius arte.
Hos ediſcit, et hos arto ſtipata theatro
Spectat Roma potens; habet hos numeratque poetas
Ad noſtrum tempus, Livi Scriptoris ab aevo.
Interdum volgus rectum videt: eſt ubi peccat.
Si veteres ita miratur laudatque poetas,
Ut nihil anteferat, nihil illis comparet; errat:

COMMENTARY.

he ſcruples not to recount ſuch of their determinations on the merit of ancient writers, as were reaſonable and well founded, as well as others, that he deemed leſs juſt, and as ſuch intended more immediately to expoſe.

We ſee then with what art the poet conducts himſelf in this attack on the *antients*, and how it ſerved his purpoſe, by turns, to ſoften and aggravate the *charge*. *Firſt*, " he wanted to lower the reputation " of the old poets." This was not to be done by general invective, or an affected diſſimulation of their juſt praiſe. He admits then [from line 63 to 66] their reaſonable pretenſions to *admiration*. It is the *degree* of it alone, to which he objects.

Si veteres ITA *miratur laudatque*, &c.

Secondly, " he wanted to draw off their applauſes from " the ancient to the modern poets." This required the *advantages* of thoſe moderns to be diſtinctly ſhewn, or, which comes to the ſame, the *comparative deficiencies* of the antients to be pointed out. Theſe were not to be diſſembled, and are, as he openly inſiſts

Si quaedam nimis antique, si pleraque dure
Dicere cedit eos, ignave multa fatetur;
Et sapit, et mecum facit, et Jove judicat aequo.
Non equidem insector, delendave carmina Laevî
Esse reor, memini quae plagosum mihi parvo
Orbilium dictare; sed emendata videri
Pulchraque, et exactis minimum distantia, miror:
Inter quae verbum emicuit si forte decorum,
Si versus paulo concinnior unus et alter;

COMMENTARY.

insists [to line 69] *obsolete language, rude and barbarous construction*, and *slovenly composition*,

> *Si quaedam nimis* ANTIQUE, *si pleraque* DURE,
> *Dicere cedit eos,* IGNAVE *multa.*

But what then? an objector replies, these were venial faults, surely; the *deficiencies* of the times, and not of the men; who, with such incorrectnesses as are here noted, might still possess the greatest *talents*, and produce the noblest *designs*. This [from line 69 to 79] is readily admitted. But, in the mean time, one thing was clear, that they were not *finished models* — *exactis minimum distantia.* Which was the main point in dispute. For the bigot's absurdity lay in this,

> *Non veniam antiquis, sed honorem et praemia posci.*

Nay, his folly is shewn to have gone still greater lengths. These boasted models of antiquity, with all their imperfections, had occasionally, [line 73, 74] though the instances were indeed rare and thinly scattered, *striking beauties.* These, under the recommendation of *age*, which, of course, commands our reve-

Injuste totum ducit venitque poema.
Indignor quicquam reprehendi, non quia crasse
Compositum, inlepideve putetur, sed quia nuper:
Nec veniam antiquis, sed honorem et praemia
posci.
Recte necne crocum floresque perambulet Attae
Fabula, si dubitem; clament periisse pudorem
Cuncti pene patres: ea cum reprehendere coner,
Quae gravis Aesopus, quae doctus Roscius egit.

COMMENTARY.

reverence, might well impose on the judgments of the *generality*, and, standing forth with advantage, as from a shaded and dark *ground*, would naturally catch the eye and admiration of the more *learned*. Thus much the poet candidly insinuates in excuse of the bigot's *ill judgment*. But, unluckily, he had cut himself off from the benefit of this plea, by avowedly grounding his *admiration*, not merely on the intrinsic excellence, so far as it went, of the ancient poetry itself; but on the advantage of any extraneous circumstance, which but casually stuck to it. The accident of a play's having passed through the mouth, and been graced by the action of a just speaker, was sufficient [from line 79 to 83] (so inexcusable were his prejudices) to attract his wonder, and justify his esteem. In so much that it became an insolence, generally cried out upon, for any one to censure such pieces of the theatre,

Quae gravis Æsopus, quae doctus Roscius egit.

This being the case, it was no longer a doubt, whether the affected admiration of antiquity proceeded

from

Vel quia nil rectum, niſi quod placuit ſibi, ducunt;
Vel quia turpe putant parere minoribus, et, quae
Inberbi didicere, ſenes perdenda fateri.
Jam Saliare Numae carmen qui laudat, et illud
Quod mecum ignorat, ſolus volt ſcire videri;

COMMENTARY.

from a deluded judgment only, or a much worſe cauſe. It could plainly be reſolved into no other, than the wilful agency of the malignant affections; which, wherever they prevail, corrupt the ſimple and ingenuous ſenſe of the mind, either, 1. [line 83] *in engendering high conceits of ſelf*, and referring all degrees of excellence to the ſuppoſed infallible ſtandard of every man's own judgment; or, 2. [to line 86] *in creating a falſe ſhame*, and reluctancy in us to be directed by the judgments of others, though *ſeen* to be more equitable, whenever they are found in oppoſition to our own rooted and preconceived opinions. The bigotry of *old men* is, eſpecially, for this reaſon, invincible. They hold themſelves upbraided by the ſharper ſight of their juniors; and regard the adoption of new ſentiments, at their years, as ſo much abſolute loſs on the ſide of the dead ſtock of their old literary poſſeſſions. Theſe conſiderations are generally of ſuch prevalency in grey veteran critics, that [from line 86 to 90] whenever, as in the caſe before us, they pretend an uncommon zeal for antiquity, and their ſagacity piques itſelf on detecting the ſuperior value of obſcure rhapſodiſts, whom nobody elſe reads, or is able to underſtand, we may be ſure the ſecret view of ſuch, is, not the generous defence and

patronage

Ingeniis non ille favet plauditque ſepultis,
Noſtra ſed impugnat, nos noſtraque lividus odit.
Quod ſi tam Graiis novitas invisa fuiſſet,
Quam nobis; quid nunc eſſet vetus? aut quid haberet,
Quod legeret tereretque viritim publicus uſus?

COMMENTARY.

patronage of *ancient* wit, but a low malevolent pleaſure in decrying the juſt pretenſions of the *modern*.

Ingeniis non ille favet plauditque ſepultis,
Noſtra ſed impugnat, nos noſtraque lividus odit.

The poet had, now, made appear the unreaſonable attachment of his countrymen to the fame of their old writers. He had thoroughly unravelled the ſophiſtical pretences, on which it affected to juſtify itſelf; and had even dared to unveil the *ſecret iniquitous principle*, from which it aroſe. It was now time to look forward to the *effects* of it; which were, in truth, very baleful; its poiſonous influences being of force to corrupt and wither, as it were, in the bud, every riſing ſpecies of excellence, and finally to check the very hopes and tendencies of true genius. Nothing can be truer than this remark; which he further enforces, and brings home to his adverſaries, by aſking a pertinent queſtion, to which it concerned them to make a ſerious reply. They had magnified, line 28, the perfection of the Greek models. But what [to line 93] if the Greeks had conceived the ſame averſion to novelties, as the Romans? How then could *theſe* models have ever been furniſhed to the public uſe? The queſtion, we ſee, inflames what was before

Ut primum positis nugari Graecia bellis
Coepit, et in vitium fortuna labier aequa;
Nunc athletarum studiis, nunc arsit equorum:
Marmoris, aut eboris fabros, aut aeris amavit;
Suspendit picta vultum mentemque tabella;
Nunc tibicinibus, nunc est gavisa tragoedis:
Sub nutrice puella velut si luderet infans,

COMMENTARY.

before affirmed to be the truth of the case; that the unrivalled excellence of the Greek poets proceeded only from long and vigorous exercise, and a painful uninterrupted application to the arts of verse. The liberal spirit of that people led them to countenance every new attempt towards superior literary excellence; and so, by the public favour, their writings, from rude essays, became at length the standard and admiration of succeeding wits. The Romans had treated their adventurers quite otherwise, and the effect was answerable. This is the purport of what to a common eye may look like a *digression* [from line 93 to 108] in which is delineated the very different genius and practice of the two nations. For the Greeks [to line 102] had applied themselves, in the intervals of their leisure from the toils of war, to the cultivation of every species of elegance, whether in *arts*, or *letters*; and loved to cherish the public emulation, by affording a free indulgence to the various and volatile disposition of the times. The activity of these restless spirits was incessantly attempting some new and untried *form* of composition; and, when *that* was brought to a due degree of perfection, it turned, *in good time*, to the cultivation of some *other*.

Quod cupide petiit, mature plena reliquit.
Quid placet, aut odio est, quod non mutabile credas?
Hoc paces habuere bonae, ventique secundi.
Romae dulce diu fuit et sollenne, reclusa
Mane domo vigilare, clienti promere jura:
Scriptos nominibus rectis expendere nummos

COMMENTARY.

Quod cupide petiit, mature plena reliquit.

So that the very caprice of *humour* [line 101] assisted, in this libertine country, to advance and help forward the public taste. Such was the effect of *peace and prosperity* with them.

Hoc paces habuere bonae ventique secundi.

Whereas the *Romans* [to line 108] by a more composed temperament and saturnine complexion had devoted their pains to the pursuit of domestic utilities, and a more dextrous management of the *arts of gain.* The consequence of which was, that when, [to line 117] by the decay of the old frugal spirit, the necessary effect of overflowing plenty and ease, they began, at length, to seek out for the elegancies of life; and *a fit of versifying*, the first of all liberal amusements, that usually seizes an idle people, had come upon them; their ignorance of rules, and want of exercise in the art of writing, rendered them wholly unfit to succeed in it. So that their awkward attempts in poetry were now as disgraceful to their *taste*, as their total disregard of it, before, had been to their *civility*. The root of this mischief was the idolatrous regard paid to their ancient poets: which unluckily, when the public emulation was so a

going,

Majores audire, minori dicere, per quae
Crescere res posset, minui damnosa libido.
Mutavit mentem populus levis, et calet uno
Scribendi studio: puerique patresque severi
Fronde comas vincti coenant, et carmina dictant.
Ipse ego, qui nullos me adfirmo scribere versus,
Invenior Parthis mendacior; et prius orto
Sole vigil, calamum et chartas et scrinia posco.
Navem agere ignarus navis timet: abrotonum aegro
Non audet, nisi qui didicit, dare: quod medicorum est,
Promittunt medici: tractant fabrilia fabri:
Scribimus indocti doctique poemata passim.

COMMENTARY.

ing, not only checked its progress, but gave it a wrong bias; and, instead of helping true genius to outstrip the lame and tardy endeavours of ancient wit, threw it aside into a vicious and unprofitable mimicry of its very imperfections. Whence it had come to pass, that, whereas in other *arts*, the previous knowledge of rules is required to the practice of them, in this of *versifying*, no such qualification was deemed necessary.

Scribimus indocti doctique poemata passim.

This mischance was *doubly* fatal to the Latin poetry. For the ill success of these blind adventurers had increased the original mischief, by confirming, as it needs must, the superstitious reverence of the old writers; and insensibly brought, as well the art

itself,

Hic error tamen et levis haec insania quantas
Virtutes habeat, sic collige: vatis avarus
Non temere est animus: versus amat, hoc studet unum;
Detrimenta, fugas servorum, incendia ridet:
Non fraudem socio, puerove incogitat ullam
Pupillo: vivit siliquis, et pane secundo:
Militiae quanquam piger et malus, utilis urbi;
Si das hoc, parvis quoque rebus magna juvari;
Os tenerum pueri balbumque poëta figurat:
Torquet ab obscoenis jam nunc sermonibus aurem;
Mox etiam pectus praeceptis format amicis,
Asperitatis et invidiae corrector et irae:

COMMENTARY.

itself, as the modern professors of it, into disrepute with the discerning public. The vindication of *both*, then, at this critical juncture, was become highly seasonable; and to this, which was the poet's main purpose, he addresses himself through the remainder of the epistle.

118 to the end. HIC ERROR TAMEN, &c.] Having sufficiently obviated the popular and reigning prejudices against the modern poets, his office of *advocate* for their fame, which he had undertaken, and was now to discharge, in form, required him to set their real merits and pretensions in a just light. He enters therefore immediately on this task. And, in drawing the character of the *true poet*, endeavours to impress the emperor with as advantageous an idea as possible, of the worth and dignity of his calling. And this, not in the fierce insulting tone of a zealot

Recte facta refert; orientia tempora notis
Instruit exemplis; inopem solatur et aegrum.
Castis cum pueris ignara puella mariti
Disceret unde preces, vatem ni Musa dedisset?
Poscit opem chorus, et praesentia numina sentit;
Caelestis implorat aquas, docta prece blandus;
Avertit morbos, metuenda pericula pellit;
Inpetrat et pacem, et locupletem frugibus annum:
Carmine Dì superi placantur, carmine Manes.

COMMENTARY.

for the *honour of his order*, which to the *great* is always disgusting, and where the occasion is, confessedly, not of the last importance, plainly absurd; but with that unpretending air of insinuation, which good sense, improved by a thorough knowledge of the world, teaches: with that seeming indifference, which disarms prejudice: in a word, with that gracious *smile in his aspect*, which his strong admirer and faint copyer, Persius, so justly noted in him, and which convinces almost without the help of argument; or, to say it more truly, *persuades* where it doth not properly *convince*. In this disposition he sets out on his defence; and yet omits no *particular*, which could any way serve to the real recommendation of *poets*, or which indeed the gravest or warmest of their friends have ever pleaded in their behalf. This defence consists [from line 118 to 139] in bringing into view their many *civil*, *moral*, and *religious* virtues. For the muse, as the poet contends, (and nothing could be more likely to conciliate the esteem of the politic emperor) administers, in this threefold capacity, to the service of the state.

But

Agricolae prisci, fortes, parvoque beati,
Condita post frumenta, levantes tempore festo
Corpus et ipsum animum spe finis dura ferentem,
Cum sociis operum pueris et conjuge fida,
Tellurem porco, Silvanum lacte piabant,
Floribus et vino Genium memorem brevis aevi.
Fescennina per hunc invecta licentia morem
Versibus alternis opprobria rustica fudit;
Libertasque recurrentis accepta per annos

COMMENTARY.

But *religion*, which was its *noblest end*, was, besides, the *first object* of poetry. The dramatic muse, in particular, had her birth, and derived her very character, from it. This circumstance then leads him with advantage, to give an historical deduction of the rise and progress of the Latin poesy, from its first rude workings in the days of barbarous superstition, through every successive period of its improvement, down to his own times. Such a view of its defects and gradual reformation, was directly to the poet's purpose. For, having magnified the virtues of his order, as of such importance to society, the question naturally occurred, by what unhappy means it had fallen out, that it was, nevertheless, in such low estimation with the public. The answer is, that the state of the Latin poetry, as yet, was very rude and imperfect: and so the public disregard was occasioned, only, by its not having attained to that degree of perfection, of which its nature was capable. Many reasons had concurred to keep the Latin poetry in this state, which he proceeds to enumerate. The *first and principal* was [from line 139 to 164] the little

 attention

Luſit amabiliter: donec jam ſaevus apertam
In rabiem coepit verti jocus, et per honeſtas
Ire domos impune minax. doluere cruento
Dente laceſſiti: fuit intactis quoque cura
Conditione ſuper communi: quin etiam lex
Poenaque lata, malo quae nollet carmine quemquam
Deſcribi. vertere modum, formidine fuſtis
Ad bene dicendum delectandumque redacti.
Graecia capta ferum victorem cepit, et artis

COMMENTARY.

attention paid *to critical learning, and the cultivation of a correct and juſt ſpirit of compoſition.* Which, again, had ariſen from the coarſe illiberal diſpoſition of the Latin muſe, who had been nurtured and brought up under the roof of rural ſuperſtition; and this, by an impure mixture of licentious jollity, had ſo corrupted her very nature, that it was only by ſlow degrees, and not till the conqueſt of Greece had imported arts and learning into Italy, that ſhe began to chaſtiſe her manners, and aſſume a juſter and more becoming deportment. And ſtill ſhe was but in the condition of a ruſtic *beauty*, when practiſing her aukward airs, and making her firſt ungracious eſſays towards a *manner.*

in longum tamen aevum
Manſerunt, hodieque manent veſtigia ruris.

Her late acquaintance with the Greek models had, indeed, improved her air, and inſpired an inclination to emulate their nobleſt graces. But how ſucceſsfully, we are given to underſtand from her unequal attempts in the two ſublimer ſpecies of their poetry, the TRAGIC, and COMIC DRAMAS.

1. [from

Intulit agreſti Latio. ſic horridus ille
Defluxit numerus Saturnius, et grave virus
Munditiae pepulere: ſed in longum tamen aevum
Manſerunt, hodieque manent, veſtigia ruris.
Serus enim Graecis admovit acumina chartis;
Et poſt Punica bella quietus quaerere coepit,
Quid Sophocles et Theſpis et Aeſchylus utile ferrent:
Tentavit quoque rem, ſi digne vertere poſſet:
Et placuit ſibi, natura ſublimis et acer.

COMMENTARY.

1. [from line 160 to 168.] *The ſtudy of the Greek tragedians* had very naturally, and to good purpoſe, in the infancy of their taſte, diſpoſed the Latin writers to *tranſlation*. Here they ſtuck long; for their tragedy, even in the Auguſtan age, was little elſe; and yet they ſucceeded but indifferently in it. The bold and animated genius of Rome was, it is readily owned, well ſuited to this work. And for force of colouring, and a truly tragic elevation, the Roman poets came not behind their great originals. But unfortunately their judgment was unformed, and they were too ſoon ſatisfied with their own productions. Strength and fire was all they endeavoured after. And with this praiſe they ſate down perfectly contented. The diſcipline of correction, the curious poliſhing of art, which had given ſuch a luſtre to the Greek tragedians, they knew nothing of; or, to ſpeak their caſe more truly, they held diſgraceful to the high ſpirit and energy of the Roman genius:

TURPEM PUTAT IN SCRIPTIS METUITQUE LITURAM.

Nam ſpirat tragicum ſatis, et feliciter audet;
Sed turpem putat inſcitus metuitque lituram.
Creditur, ex medio quia res arceſſit, habere
Sudoris minimum; ſed habet comoedia tanto
Plus oneris, quanto veniae minus. aſpice, Plautus
Quo pacto partis tutetur amantis ephebi: * / 2
Ut patris attenti, lenonis ut inſidioſi:
Quantus ſit Doſſennus edacibus in paraſitis:
Quam non adſtricto percurrat pulpita ſocco.
Geſtit enim nummum in loculos demittere; poſt hoc

COMMENTARY.

2. It did not fare better with them [from line 168 to 175] in their attempts to rival *the Greek comedy*. They prepoſterouſly ſet out with the notion of its being eaſier to execute this drama than the tragic: whereas, to hit its genuine character with exactneſs, was, in truth, a point of much more difficulty. As the *ſubject* of comedy was taken from common life, they ſuppoſed an ordinary degree of care might ſuffice to do it juſtice. No wonder, then, they overlooked, or never came up to, that nice adjuſtment of the *manners*, that truth and decorum of *character*, wherein the glory of comic painting conſiſts, and which none but the quickeſt eye can diſcern, and the ſteddieſt hand execute; and, in the room, amuſed us with *high colouring*, and *falſe drawing*; with *extravagant, aggravated portraitures*; which, neglecting the modeſt proportion of real life, are the certain arguments of an unpractiſed pencil, or vicious taſte.

What

Securus, cadat an recto stet fabula talo.
Quem tulit ad scenam ventoso gloria curru,
Exanimat lentus spectator, sedulus inflat.
Sic leve, sic parvum est, animum quod laudis avarum
Subruit ac reficit. valeat res ludicra, si me
Palma negata macrum, donata reducit opimum.
Saepe, etiam audacem, fugat hoc terretque poetam;

COMMENTARY.

What contributed to this prostitution of the comic muse, was [to line 177] the seducement of that corruptress of all virtue, *the love of money*; which had thoroughly infected the Roman wits, and was, in fact, the sole object of their pains. Hence, provided they could but catch the applauses of the people, to which the pleasantry of the comic scene more especially aspires, and so secure a good round *price* from the magistrates, whose office it was to furnish this kind of entertainment, they became indifferent to every nobler view and honester purpose. In particular [to line 182] they so little considered *fame and the praise of good writing*, that they made it the ordinary topic of their ridicule; representing it as the mere illusion of vanity, and the pitiable infirmity of *lean-witted* minds, to be catched by the lure of so empty and unsubstantial a benefit.

Though, were any one, in defiance of public ridicule, so *daring* (as there is no occasion in life, which calls for, or demonstrates a greater firmness) as frankly to avow and submit himself to this generous *motive*, the surest inspirer of every virtuous excellence, yet one thing remained to check and weaken the vigour of his emulation. This [from line 182 to 187]

Quod numero plures, virtute et honore minores,
Indocti, stolidique, et depugnare parati 184
Si discordet eques, media inter carmina poscunt
Aut ursum aut pugiles: his nam plebecula gaudet.
Verum equiti quoque jam migravit ab aure voluptas
Omnis, ad ingratos oculos, et gaudia vana.
Quatuor aut pluris aulaea premuntur in horas;

COMMENTARY.

was the folly and ill taste of the undiscerning multitude; who, in all countries, have a great share in determining the fate and character of scenical representations, but, from the popular constitution of the government, were, at Rome, of the first consequence. These, by their rude clamours, and the authority of their numbers, were enough to dishearten the most intrepid genius; when, after all his endeavours to reap the glory of an absolute work, the action was almost sure to be mangled and broken in upon by the shews of *wild beasts and gladiators*; those *dear delights*, which the Romans, it seems, prized much above the highest pleasures of the drama.

Nay, the poet's case was still more desperate. For it was not the untutored rabble, as in other countries, that gave a countenance to these illiberal sports: even *rank and quality*, at Rome, debased itself in shewing the fiercest passion for these *shews*, and was as ready, as abject commonalty itself, to prefer the uninstructing pleasures of the *eye* to those of the *ear*.

EQUITI *quoque jam migravit ab aure voluptas*
Omnis ad ingratos oculos et gaudia vana.

And,

Dum fugiunt equitum turmae, peditumque catervae:
Mox trahitur manibus regum fortuna retortis:
Eſſeda feſtinant, pilenta, petorrita, naves:
Captivum portatur ebur, captiva Corinthus.
Si foret in terris, rideret Democritus; ſeu
Diverſum confuſa genus panthera camelo,
Sive elephas albus volgi converterit ora:

COMMENTARY.

And, becauſe this barbarity of taſte had contributed more than any thing elſe to deprave the poetry of the ſtage, and diſcourage its beſt maſters from ſtudying its perfection, what follows [from line 189 to 207] is intended, in all the keenneſs of raillery, to ſatirize this madneſs. It afforded an ample field for the poet's ridicule. For, beſides the riotous diſorders of their theatre, the ſenſeleſs admiration of *pomp and ſpectacle* in their plays had ſo enchanted his countrymen, that the very decorations of the ſcene, the tricks and trappings of the comedians, were ſurer to catch the applauſes of the gaping multitude, than any regard to the juſtneſs of the poet's deſign, or the beauty of his execution.

Here the poet ſhould naturally have concluded his *defence of the dramatic writers*; having alledged every thing in their favour, that could be urged, plauſibly, from *the ſtate of the Roman ſtage: the genius of the people: and the ſeveral prevailing practices of ill taſte*, which had brought them into diſrepute with the beſt judges. But finding himſelf obliged, in the courſe of this vindication of the modern *ſtage-poets*, to cenſure, as ſharply as their very enemies, the vices and

Spectaret populum ludis attentius ipſis,
Ut ſibi præbentem mimo ſpectacula plura:
Scriptores autem narrare putaret aſello
Fabellam ſurdo. nam quae pervincere voces
Evaluere ſonum, referunt quem noſtra theatra?
Garganum mugire putes nemus, aut mare Tuſcum.
Tanto cum ſtrepitu ludi ſpectantur, et artes,
Divitiaeque peregrinae: quibus oblitus actor
Cum ſtetit in ſcena, concurrit dextera laevae:
Dixit adhuc aliquid? nil ſane. quid placet ergo?
Lana Tarentino violas imitata veneno.
Ac ne forte putes me, quae facere ipſe recuſem,

COMMENTARY.

defects of their *poetry*; and fearing leſt this ſeverity on a ſort of writing, to which himſelf had never pretended, might be miſinterpreted as the effect of envy only, and a malignant diſpoſition towards the art itſelf, under cover of pleading for its *profeſſors*, he therefore frankly avows [from line 208 to 214] his preference of the *dramatic*, to every other ſpecies of poetry; declaring the ſovereignty of its pathos over the *affections*, and the magic of its illuſive ſcenery on the *imagination*, to be the higheſt argument of poetic excellence, the laſt and nobleſt exerciſe of the human genius.

One thing ſtill remained. He had taken upon himſelf to apologize for the Roman poets in *general*; as may be ſeen from the large terms, in which he propoſes his ſubject.

Hic error tamen et levis haec inſania quantas
Virtutes habeat, ſic collige.

But

Cum recte tractent alii laudare maligne:
Ille per extentum funem mihi posse videtur
Ire poeta; meum qui pectus inaniter angit,
Inritat, mulcet, falsis terroribus inplet,
Ut magus; et modo me Thebis, modo ponit Athenis.
Verum age, et his, qui se lectori credere malunt,
Quam spectatoris fastidia ferre superbi,
Curam impende brevem: si munus Apolline dignum
Vis complere libris; et vatibus addere calcar,
Ut studio majore petant Helicona virentem.

COMMENTARY.

But, after a general encomium on the *office* itself, he confines his defence to the *writers for the stage* only. In conclusion then, he was constrained, by the very purpose of his address, to say a word or two in behalf of the remainder of this neglected family; of those, who, as the poet expresses it, had *rather trust to the equity of the closet, than subject themselves to the caprice and insolence of the theatre*.

Now, as before, in asserting the honour of the stage-poets, he every-where supposes the emperor's *disgust* to have sprung from the wrong conduct of the poets themselves, and then extenuates the blame of such *conduct*, by considering, still further, the *causes* which gave rise to it; so he prudently observes the like method here. The politeness of his address concedes to Augustus, the just *offence* he had taken to his brother poets; whose honour, however, he contrives to save, by softening the *occasions* of it. This is the drift of what follows [from line 214 to 229] where

4 he

Multa quidem nobis [illegible]mus mala ſaepe poëtae,
(Ut vineta egomet caedam mea) [illegible] tibi librum
Sollicito damus, aut feſſo: cum laedimur, [illegible]
Si quis amicorum eſt auſus reprendere verſum:
Cum loca jam recitata revolvimus inrevocati:
Cum lamentamur non adparere labores
Noſtros, et tenui deducta poemata filo:

COMMENTARY.

he pleaſantly recounts the ſeveral foibles and indiſcretions of the muſe; but in a way, that could only diſpoſe the emperor to ſmile at, or at moſt to pity, her infirmities, not provoke his ſerious cenſure and diſeſteem. They amount, on the whole, but to certain idleneſſes of *vanity*, the almoſt inſeparable attendants of *wit*, as well as *beauty*; and may be forgiven in *each*, as implying a ſtrong *deſire* of pleaſing, or rather as *qualifying* both to pleaſe. One of the moſt exceptionable of theſe *vanities* was a fond perſuaſion, too readily taken up by men of parts and genius, that *preferment is the conſtant pay of merit*; and that, from the moment their talents become known to the public, diſtinction and advancement are ſure to follow. They believed, in ſhort, they had only to convince the world of their ſuperior abilities, to deſerve the favour and countenance of their prince. But fond and preſumptuous as theſe hopes are (continues the poet [from line 229 to 244] with all the inſinuation of a courtier, and yet with a becoming ſenſe of the dignity of his own character) it may deſerve a ſerious conſideration, what poets are fit to be entruſted with the glory of princes; what *miniſters* are worth retaining

Cum ſperamus eo rem venturam, ut, ſimul atque
Carmina reſcieris nos fingere, commodus ultro
Arceſſas, et egere vetes, et ſcribere cogas.
Sed tamen eſt operae pretium cognoſcere, qualis
Aedituos habeat belli ſpectata domique
Virtus, indigno non committenda poetae.
Gratus Alexandro regi Magno fuit ille

COMMENTARY.

ing in the ſervice of an illuſtrious VIRTUE, whoſe honours demand to be ſolemnized with a religious reverence, and ſhould not be left to the profanation of vile, unhallowed hands. And, to ſupport the authority of this remonſtrance, he alledges the example of a great monarch, who had diſhonoured himſelf by a neglect of this care; of ALEXANDER THE GREAT, who, when maſter of the world, as Auguſtus now was, perceived, indeed, the importance of gaining a poet to his ſervice; but unluckily choſe ſo ill, that his encomiums (as muſt ever be the caſe with a vile panegyriſt) but tarniſhed the native ſplendor of thoſe virtues, which his office required him to preſent, in their fulleſt and faireſt glory, to the admiration of the world. In his appointment of *artiſts*, whoſe ſkill is, alſo, highly ſerviceable to the fame of princes, he ſhewed a truer judgment. For he ſuffered none but an APELLES and a LYSIPPUS to counterfeit the form and faſhion of his *perſon*. But his *taſte*, which was thus exact, and even *ſubtile* in what concerned the mechanic execution of the *fine arts*, took up with a CHOERILUS, to tranſmit an image of his *mind* to future ages; ſo groſly undiſcerning was he in works of poetry, and the liberal *offerings of the muſe!*

And

Choerilos, incultis qui versibus et male natis
Rettulit acceptos, regale nomisma, Philippos.
Sed veluti tractata notam labemquè remittunt
Atramenta, fere scriptores carmine foedo
Splendida facta linunt. idem rex ille, poëma
Qui tam ridiculum tam care prodigus emit,
Edicto vetuit; ne quis se, praeter Apellen
Pingeret, aut alius Lysippo cuderet aera
Fortis Alexandri voltum simulantia. quod si
Judicium subtile videndis artibus illud
Ad libros et ad haec Musarum dona vocares;
Boeotum in crasso jurares aëre natum.
At neque dedecorant tua de se judicia, atque

COMMENTARY.

And thus the poet makes a double use of the ill judgment of this imperial critic. For nothing could better demonstrate the importance of *poetry* to the honour of *greatness*, than that this illustrious conqueror, without any particular knowledge or discernment in the *art* itself, should think himself concerned to court its assistance. And, then, what could be more likely to engage the emperor's further protection and love of *poetry*, than the insinuation (which is made with infinite address) that, as he honoured it equally, so he understood its merits much better? For [from line 245 to 248, where, by a beautiful concurrence, the flattery of his prince falls in with the honester purpose of doing justice to the memory of his friends] it was not the same unintelligent liberality, which had cherished Choerilus, that poured the full stream of Caesar's bounty

Munera, quae multa dantis cum laude tulerunt
Dilecti tibi Virgilius Variusque poetae:
Nec magis expressi voltus per aënea signa,
Quam per vatis opus mores animique virorum
Clarorum adparent. nec sermones ego mallem
Repentis per humum, quam res componere gestas,
Terrarumque situs, et flumina dicere, et arcis
Montibus impositas, et barbara regna, tuisque
Auspiciis totum confecta duella per orbem,
Claustraque custodem pacis cohibentia Janum,
Et formidatam Parthis, te principe, Romam:
Si quantum cuperem, possem quoque. sed neque
parvum

COMMENTARY.

bounty on such persons, as VARIUS and VIRGIL. And, as if the spirit of these inimitable poets had, at once, seized him, he breaks away in a bolder run of verse [from line 248 to 250] *to sing the triumphs of an art*, which expressed the *manners and the mind* in fuller and more durable *relief*, than painting, or even sculpture, had ever been able to give to the external *figure*: And [from line 250 to the end] *apologizes for himself* in adopting the humbler epistolary *species*, when a warmth of inclination and the unrivaled glories of his prince were continually urging him on to the nobler, *encomiastic* poetry. His excuse, in brief, is taken from the conscious inferiority of his genius, and a tenderness for the fame of the emperor, which is never more disserved than by the officious sedulity of bad poets to do it honour. And with this apology, one while condescending to the
unfeigned

Carmen majeſtas recipit tua: nec meus audet
Rem tentare pudor, quam vires ferre recuſent.
Sedulitas autem ſtulte, quem diligit, urguet;
Praecipue cum ſe numeris commendat et arte.
Diſcit enim citius, meminitque libentius illud
Quod quis deridet, quam quod probat et veneratur.
Nil moror officium, quod me gravat: ac neque ficto
In pejus voltu proponi cereus uſquam,
Nec prave factis decorari verſibus opto:
Ne rubeam pingui donatus munere, et una
Cum ſcriptore meo capſa porrectus operta,
Deferar in vicum vendentem thus et odores,
Et piper, et quicquid chartis amicitur ineptis.

COMMENTARY.

unfeigned humility of a perſon, ſenſible of the *kind and meaſure* of his abilities, and then, again, ſuſtaining itſelf by a freedom, and even familiarity, which real merit knows, on certain occaſions, to take without offence, the epiſtle concludes.

If the general opinion may be truſted, this, which was one of the *laſt*, is alſo among the *nobleſt*, of the great poet's compoſitions. Perhaps, the reader, who conſiders it in the plain and ſimple order, to which the foregoing analyſis hath reduced it, may ſatisfy himſelf, that this praiſe hath not been undeſervedly beſtowed.

NOTES

NOTES

ON THE

EPISTLE TO AUGUSTUS.

NOTES

ON THE

EPISTLE TO AUGUSTUS.

EPISTOLA AD AUGUSTUM.] The epistle to AUGUSTUS is *an apology for the Roman poets*. The epistle to the PISOS, *a criticism on their poetry*. *This* to Augustus may be therefore considered as a sequel of *that* to the Pisos; and which could not well be omitted; for the author's design of forwarding the study and improvement of the *art of poetry* required him to bespeak the public favour to its *professors*.

But as, *there*, in correcting the abuses of their poetry, he mixes, occasionally, some encomiums on *poets*; so, *here*, in pleading the cause of the poets, we find him interweaving instructions on *poetry*. Which was but according to the writer's *occasions* in each work. For the freedom of his censure on the *art of poetry* was to be softened by some expressions of his good-will towards the poets; and this apology for *their fame* had been too direct and unmanaged, but for the qualifying appearance of its intending the further benefit of the *art*. The coincidence, then, of the ſame general *method*, as well as *deſign*, in the two epiſtles, made it not improper to give them together, and on the ſame ſooting, to the public. Though both the *ſubject* and *method* of this laſt are ſo clear as to make a continued commentary upon it much leſs wanted.

4. Si longo sermone morer tua tempora, Caesar.] The poet is thought to begin with apologizing for the *ſhortneſs of this epiſtle*. And yet it is one of the longeſt he ever wrote. How is this inconſiſtency to be reconciled? " Horace parle pêut être ainſi pour ne pas " rebûter Auguſte, et pour lui faire connôitre, " qu'il auroit fait une lettre, beaucoup plus " longue, s'il avoit ſuivi ſon inclination." This is the beſt account of the matter we have, hitherto, been able to come at. But the familiar civility of ſuch a compliment, as M. Dacier ſuppoſes, though it might be well enough to an *equal*, or, if dreſſed up in ſpruce phraſes, might make a figure in the *lettres familieres et galantes* of his own nation; yet is ſurely of a caſt entirely foreign to the Roman gravity, more eſpecially in an addreſs to the emperor of the world. Mr. Pope, perceiving the abſurdity of the common interpretation, ſeems to have read the lines

interro-

interrogatively; which, though it saves the sense, and suits the purpose of the English poet very well, yet neither agrees with the language nor serious air of the original. The case, I believe, was this. The genius of epistolary writing demands, that the subject-matter be not abruptly delivered, or hastily obtruded on the person addressed; but, as the law of decorum prescribes (for the rule holds in *writing*, as in *conversation*), be gradually and respectfully introduced to him. This obtains more particularly in applications to the *great*, and on important subjects. But, now, the poet, being to address his prince on a point of no small delicacy, and on which he foresaw he should have occasion to hold him pretty long, prudently contrives to get, as soon as possible, into his subject; and, to that end, hath the art to convert the very transgression of this rule into the justest and most beautiful compliment.

That cautious preparation, which is ordinarily requisite in our approaches to *greatness*, had been, the poet observes, in the present case, highly unseasonable, as the business and interests of the empire must, in the mean time, have stood still and been suspended. By *sermone* then we are to understand, not the *body* of the epistle, but the proeme or *introduction* only. The *body*, as of public concern, might be allowed to engage, at full length, the emperor's attention. But the *introduction*, consisting of *ceremonial* only, the *common good* required him to shorten as much as possible. It was no time for using an insignificant preamble, or, in our English phrase, of making *long speeches*. The reason, too, is founded, not merely in the elevated rank of the emperor, but in the peculiar diligence and sollicitude, with which, history tells us, he endeavoured to promote, by various ways, the interests of his country. So that the compliment is as *just* as it is *polite*. It may be further observed, that *sermo* is used in Horace, to signify the ordinary style of conversation. [See Sat. i. 3. 65. and iv. 42.] and therefore not improperly denotes the familiarity of the epistolary address, which, in its easy expression, so nearly approaches to it.

13. Urit enim fulgore suo, qui praegravat artes Infra se positas: extinctus amabitur idem.] The poet, we may suppose, spoke this from experience. And so might another of later date when he complained:

Unhappy Wit, like most mistaken things,
Atones not for that envy which it brings.

Essay on Crit. ver. 494.

Unless it be thought, that, as this was said by him very early in life, it might rather pass for a prediction of his future fortunes. Be this as it

will,

will, the sufferings, which *unhappy wit* is conceived to bring on itself from the *envy*, it excites, are, I am apt to think, somewhat aggravated; at least if one may judge from the effects it had on this *complainant*. That which would be likely to afflict him most, was the *envy* of his friends. But the generosity of these deserves to be recorded. The *wits* took no offence at his fame, till they found it eclipse their *own*: And his *philosopher and guide*, it is well known, stuck close to him, till another and brighter star had gotten the ascendant. Or, supposing there might be some malice in the case, it is plain there was little mischief. And for this little the poet's creed provides an ample recompence. EXTINCTUS AMABITUR IDEM: not, we may be sure, by *those* he most improved, enlightened, and obliged; but by late impartial posterity; and by ONE at least of his surviving friends, who generously took upon him the patronage of his fame, and who inherits his genius and his virtues.

14. EXTINCTUS AMABITUR IDEM.] *Envy*, says a discerning antient, *is the vice of those, who are too weak to contend, and too proud to submit: vitium eorum, qui nec cedere volunt, nec possunt contendere* [a]. Which, while it sufficiently exposes the folly and malignity of this hateful

[a] Quinctilian, lib. xi. c. 1.

passion, secures the honour of human nature; as implying at the same time, that its worst corruptions are not without a mixture of generosity in them. For this false pride in *refusing to submit*, though absurd and mischievous enough, when unsupported by all *ability to contend*, yet discovers such a sense of superior excellence, as shews, how difficult it is for human nature to divest itself of all virtue. Accordingly, when the too powerful *splendor* is withdrawn, our natural veneration of it takes place: *Extinctus amabitur idem*. This is the true exposition of the poet's sentiment; which therefore appears just the reverse of what his French interpreter would fix upon him. "La justice, que nous "rendons aux grands hommes après leur mort, "ne vient pas de l'AMOUR, que nous avons pour "leur *vertu*, mais de la HAINE, dont notre cœur "est rempli pour ceux, qui ont pris leur PLACE." An observation, which only becomes the misanthropy of an old cynic virtue, or the selfishness of a modern system of ethics.

15. PRAESENTI TIBI MATUROS, &c. to line 18.] We are not to wonder at this and the like extravagances of adulation in the Augustan poets. They had ample authority for what they did of this sort. We know, that altars were erected to the emperor by the command of the senate; and

and that he was publickly invoked, as an establiſhed, tutelary divinity. But the ſeeds of the corruption had been ſown much earlier. For we find it ſprung up, or rather (as of all the ill weeds, which the teeming ſoil of human depravity throws forth, none is more thriving and grows faſter than this of *flattery*) flouriſhing at its height, in the tyranny of J. CAESAR. Balbus, in a letter to Cicero, [Ep. ad Att. l. ix.] *ſwears by the health and ſafety of Cæſar: ità incolumi Caeſare, moriar.* And Dio tells us [l. xliv.] that it was, by the expreſs injunction of the ſenate, decreed, even in Caeſar's life-time, that the Romans ſhould bind themſelves by this oath. The ſenate alſo, as we learn from the ſame writer, [l. xliii.] upon receiving the news of his defeat of Pompey's ſons, cauſed his ſtatue to be ſet up, in the temple of Romulus, with this inſcription, DEO INVICTO [*b*].

It is true, theſe and ſtill greater honours had been long paid to the Roman governors in their

[*b*] Θεῷ ἀνικήτῳ ἐπιγράψαντες. Though, to complete the farce, it was with the greateſt ſhyneſs and reluctance, that the humility of theſe lords of the univerſe could permit itſelf to accept the enſigns of deity, as the court-hiſtorians of thoſe times are forward to inform us. An affectation, which was thought to fit ſo well upon them, that we find it afterwards practiſed, in the abſurdeſt and moſt impudent manner, by the worſt of their ſucceſſors.

provinces,

provinces, by the *abject, slavish Asiatics*. And this, no doubt, facilitated the admission of such idolatries into the capital [*c*]. But that a people, from the highest notions of an independent republican equality, could so soon be brought to this prostrate adoration of their first *lord*, is perfectly amazing! In this, they shewed themselves ripe for servitude. Nothing could keep them out of the hands of a master. And one can scarcely read such accounts as these, without condemning the vain efforts of dying patriotism, which laboured so fruitlessly, may one not almost say, so weakly? to protract the liberty of such a people. Who can, after this, wonder at the incense, offered up by a few court-poets? The adulation of Virgil, which has given so much offence, and of Horace, who keeps pace with him, was, we see, but the authorized language of the times; presented indeed with address, but without the heightenings and privileged licence of their profession. For, to their credit, it must be owned, that, though in the office of *poets*, they were to comply with the popular voice, and echo it back to the ears of sovereignty; yet, as *men*, they had too much good sense, and too scrupulous a regard to the

[*c*] See a learned and accurate dissertation on the subject in HIST. DE L'ACAD. DES INSCR. &c. tom. i.

dignity of their characters, to exaggerate and go beyond it.

It should, in all reason, surprize and disgust us still more, that modern writers have not always shewn themselves so discrete. The grave and learned LIPSIUS was not ashamed, even without the convenient pretext of popular flattery, or poetic *colouring*, in so many words, to make a god of his patron: who, though neither king, nor pope, was yet the next best material for this manufacture, an archbishop. For, though the critic knew, that it was *not every wood that will make a Mercury*, yet nobody would dispute the fitness of that, which grew so near the altar. In plain words, I am speaking of an archbishop of MECHLIN, whom, after a deal of fulsome compliment (which was the vice of the man), he exalts at last, with a pagan complaisance, into the order of deities. "Ad haec," says he, "erga omnes humanitas et facilitas me "faciunt, ut omnes te non tanquàm hominem "aliquem de nostro coetu, sed tanquam DEUM "QUENDAM DE COELO DELAPSUM INTUEAN-"TUR ET ADMIRENTUR."

16. JURANDASQUE TUUM PER NUMEN PONIMUS ARAS.] On this idea of the APOTHEOSIS, which was the usual mode of flattery in the Augustan age, but, as having the countenance

of

of public authority, ſometimes inartificially enough employed, Virgil hath projected one of the nobleſt allegories in ancient poetry, and at the ſame time hath given to it all the force of *juſt* compliment, the *occaſion* itſelf allowed. *Each* of theſe excellencies was to be expected from his talents. For, as his genius led him to the *ſublime*; ſo his exquiſite judgment would inſtruct him to palliate this bold fiction, and qualify, as much as poſſible, the ſhocking adulation, implied in it. So ſingular a beauty deſerves to be ſhewn at large.

The *third* GEORGIC ſets out with an apology for the low and ſimple argument of that work, which, yet, the poet eſteemed, for its novelty, preferable to the ſublimer, but trite, themes of the Greek writers. Not but he intended, on ſome future occaſion, to adorn a nobler ſubject. This was the great plan of the Aeneïs, which he now *prefigures* and unfolds at large. For, taking advantage of the nobleſt privilege of his *art*, he breaks away, in a fit of *prophetic* enthuſiaſm, to fortel his ſucceſſes in this projected enterprize, and, under the imagery of the ancient *triumph*, which comprehends, or ſuggeſts to the imagination, whatever is moſt auguſt in human affairs, to delineate the future glories of this ambitious deſign. The whole conception, as we ſhall ſee, is of the utmoſt grandeur and magni-

magnificence; though, according to the usual management of the poet (which, as not being apprehended by his critics, hath furnished occasion, even to the best of them, to charge him with a want of the *sublime*) he hath contrived to soften and *familiarize* its appearance to the reader, by the artful manner in which it is introduced. It stands thus:

tentanda via est, qua me quoque possim
Tollere humo, VICTORQUE *virûm volitare per ora.*

This idea of *victory*, thus casually dropped, he makes the basis of his imagery; which, by means of this gradual preparation, offers itself easily to the apprehension, though it thereby loses, as the poet designed it should, much of that broad *glare*, in which writers of less judgment love to shew their ideas, as tending to set the common reader at a gaze. The allegory then proceeds:

Primus ego patriam mecum (modo vita supersit)
Aonio rediens deducam vertice Musas.

The projected conquest was no less than that of all the *Grecian Muses* at once; whom, to carry on the decorum of the allegory, he threatens, 1. to force from their high and advantageous situation on the summit of the *Aonian mount*; and, 2. bring *captive* with him into Italy: the *former* circumstance intimating to us the difficulty

ficulty and danger of the enterprize; and the *latter*, his complete execution of it.

The *palmy*, triumphal entry, which was usual to victors on their return from foreign successes, follows:

Primus Idumaeas referam tibi, Mantua, palmas.

But ancient conquerors did not hold it sufficient to reap this transient fruit of their labours. They were ambitious to consecrate their glory to immortality, by a *temple*, or other public monument, which was to be built out of the spoils of the conquered cities or countries. This, the reader sees, is suitable to the idea of the great work proposed; which was, out of the old remains of Grecian art, to compose a *new* one, that should comprize the virtues of them all: as, in fact, the Aeneïd is known to unite in itself whatever is most excellent, not in Homer only, but, universally, in the wits of Greece. The everlasting monument of the *marble* temple is then reared:

Et viridi in campo templum de MARMORE *ponam.*

And, because ancient superstition usually preferred, for these purposes, the banks of *rivers* to other situations, therefore the poet, in beautiful allusion to the site of some of the most celebrated pagan temples, builds *his* on the MINCIUS. We see

see with what a scrupulous propriety the allusion is carried on:

> *Propter aquam, tardis ingens ubi flexibus errat*
> MINCIUS, *et tenera praetexit arundine ripas.*

Next, this temple was to be dedicated, as a monument of the victor's *piety*, as well as glory, to some propitious, tutelary deity, under whose auspices the great adventure had been atchieved. The *dedication* is then made to the poet's *divinity*, Augustus:

> *In medio mihi* CAESAR *erit, templumque tenebit.*

TEMPLUM TENEBIT. The expression is emphatical; as intimating to us, and prefiguring the secret purpose of the Aeneis, which was, in the person of Aeneas, to shadow forth and consecrate the character of Augustus. His divinity was to fill and *occupy* that great work. And the ample circuit of the epic plan was projected only, as a more awful enclosure of that august presence, which was to *inhabit* and solemnize the vast round of this poetic building.

And now the wonderful address of the poet's artifice appears. The mad servility of his country had *deified* the emperor in good earnest: and his brother poets made no scruple to *worship* in his temples, and to come before him with handfuls of *real* incense, smoking from the altars. But the sobriety of Virgil's adoration was of another

another cast. He seizes this circumstance only to *embody* a poetical fiction; which, on the supposition of an actual *deification*, hath all the force of compliment, which the *fact* implies, and yet, as presented through the chaste veil of allegory, eludes the offence, which the *naked* recital must needs have given to sober and reasonable men. Had the emperor's *popular* divinity been flatly acknowledged and adored, the praise, even under Virgil's management, had been insufferable for its extravagance; and, without some support for his poetical *numen* to rest upon, the figure had been more forced and strained, than the rules of just writing allow. As it is, the historical truth of his *apotheosis* authorizes and supports the *fiction*; and the fiction, in its turn, serves to refine and palliate the *history*.

The Aeneïs being, by the poet's improvement of this circumstance, thus naturally predicted under the image of a *temple*, we may expect to find a close and studied analogy betwixt them. The great, component parts of the *one* will, no doubt, be made, very faithfully, to represent and adumbrate those of the *other*. This hath been executed with great art and diligence.

1. The *temple*, we observed, was erected on the banks of a river. This site was not only proper, for the reason already mentioned, but

alſo, for the further convenience of inſtituting *public games*, the ordinary attendants of the *conſecration* of temples. Theſe were generally, as in the caſe of the Olympic, and others, celebrated on the banks of rivers.

Illi victor ego, et Tyrio conſpectus in oſtro,
Centum quadrijuges agitabo ad flumina currus.
Cuncta mihi, Alpheum linquens lucoſque Molorchi,
Curſibus et crudo decernet Graecia caeſtu.

To ſee the propriety of the *figure* in this place, the reader needs only be reminded of the *book of games* in the Aeneïd, which was purpoſely introduced in honour of the emperor, and not, as is commonly thought, for a mere trial of ſkill between the poet and his maſter. The emperor was paſſionately fond of theſe ſports, and was even the author, or reſtorer, of *one* of them. It is not to be doubted, that he alludes alſo to the *quinquennial games*, actually celebrated, in honour of his temples, through many parts of the empire. And this the poet undertakes in the *civil* office of VICTOR.

2. What follows is in the *religious* office of PRIEST. For it is to be noted, that, in aſſuming this double character, which the decorum of the ſolemnities, here recounted, preſcribed, the poet has an eye to the *political* deſign of the Aeneïs, which was to do honour to Caeſar, in

either capacity of a *civil* and *religious* perſonage; both being eſſential to the idea of the PERFECT LEGISLATOR, whoſe office and character (as an eminent critic hath lately ſhewn us [*d*], it was his purpoſe, in this immortal work, to adorn and recommend. The account of his *ſacerdotal functions* is delivered in theſe words:

Ipſe caput tonſae foliis ornatus olivae
Dona feram. Jam nunc ſolemnes ducere pompas
Ad delubra juvat, caeſoſque videre juvencos;
Vel ſcena ut verſis diſcedat frontibus, utque
Purpurea intexti tollant aulaea Britanni.

The imagery in this place cannot be underſtood, without reflecting on the cuſtomary form and diſpoſition of the pagan temples. DELUBRUM, or DELUBRA, for either *number* is uſed indifferently, denotes the ſhrine, or ſanctuary, wherein the ſtatue of the preſiding god was placed. This was in the center of the building. Exactly before the *delubrum*, and at no great diſtance from it, was the ALTAR. Further, the ſhrine, or *delubrum*, was incloſed and ſhut up on all ſides by *doors* of curious carved work, and ductile *veils*, embelliſhed by the rich embroidery of *flowers*, *animals*, or *human figures*. This being obſerved, the progreſs of the imagery before us will be this. The proceſſion

[*d*] DIV. LEG. vol. i. B. ii. S. 4.

ad delubra, or ſhrine: the ſacrifice on the *altars*, erected before it: and, laſtly, the painted, or rather wrought *ſcenery* of the purple *veils*, incloſing the image, which were ornamented, and ſeemed to be ſuſtained, or held up by the figures of *inwoven Britons*. The meaning of all which is, that the poet would proceed to the celebration of Caeſar's praiſe in all the gradual, ſolemn preparation of poetic pomp: that he would render the moſt grateful *offerings* to his divinity in thoſe occaſional *epiſodes*, which he ſhould conſecrate to his more immediate honour: and, finally, that he would provide the richeſt texture of his fancy, for a covering to that admired *image* of his virtues, which was to make the ſovereign pride and glory of his poem. The choice of the *inwoven Britons*, for the ſupport of his *veil*, is well accounted for by thoſe who tell us, that Auguſtus was proud to have a number of theſe to ſerve about him in quality of ſlaves.

The ornaments of the DOORS of this *delubrum*, on which the ſculptor uſed to laviſh all the riches of his *art*, are next delineated.

In foribus pugnam ex auro ſolidoque elephanto
Gangaridum faciam, victoriſque arma Quirini;
Atque hic undantem bello, magnumque fluentem
Nilum, ac navali ſurgentes aere columnas.
Addam urbes Aſiae domitas, pulſumque Niphatem,
Fidentemque fugâ Parthum verſiſque ſagittis;

Et duo rapta manu diverſo ex hoſte trophaea,
Biſque triumphatas utroque ex littore gentes.

Here the covering of the *figure* is too thin to hide the *literal* meaning from the commoneſt reader, who ſees, that the ſeveral triumphs of Caeſar, here recorded in *ſculpture*, are thoſe, which the poet hath taken moſt pains to *finiſh*, and hath occaſionally inſerted, as it were, in *miniature*, in ſeveral places of his *poem*. Let him only turn to the prophetic ſpeech of Anchiſes's ſhade in the VIth, and to the deſcription of the ſhield in the VIIIth book.

Hitherto we have contemplated the decorations of the *ſhrine*, i. e. ſuch as bear a more direct and immediate reference to the honour of Caeſar. We are now preſented with a view of the remoter, ſurrounding ornaments of the temple. Theſe are the illuſtrious Trojan chiefs, whoſe ſtory was to furniſh the materials, or, more properly, to form the body and *caſe*, as it were, of his auguſt ſtructure. They are alſo connected with the idol deity of the place by the cloſeſt ties of relationſhip, the Julian family affecting to derive its pedigree from this proud original. The poet then, in his arrangement of theſe additional figures, with admirable judgment, completes and rounds the entire fiction.

Stabunt

Stabunt et Parii lapides, spirantia signa,
Assaraci proles, demissaeque ab Jove gentis
Nomina: Trosque parens et Trojae Cynthius auctor.

Nothing now remains but for *fame* to eternize the glories of what the great architect had, at the expence of so much art and labour, completed; which is predicted in the highest sublime of ancient poetry, under the idea of ENVY, whom the poet personalizes, shuddering at the view of such transcendent perfection; and tasting, beforehand, the pains of a remediless vexation, strongly pictured in the image of the worst, infernal tortures.

INVIDIA *infelix furias amnemque severum*
Cocyti metuet, tortosque Ixionis angues,
Immanemque rotam, et non exuperabile saxum.

Thus have I presumed, but with a religious awe, to inspect and declare the mysteries of this ideal temple. The attempt after all might have been censured, as prophane, if the great *Mystagogue* himself, or somebody for him [*e*], had

[*e*] In these lines,

Mox tamen ardentes accingar dicere pugnas
Caesaris, et nomen famâ tot ferre per annos,
Tithoni primâ quot abest ab origine Caesar.

Which I suspect not to have been from the hand of Virgil. And,

I. On account of some *peculiarities in the expression.*

1. *Accingar* is of frequent use in the best authors,

 not

not given us the undoubted key to it. Under this encouragement, I could not withstand the

to denote *a readiness and resolution to do any thing*; but as joined with an *infinitive mood*, *accingar dicere*, I do not remember to have ever seen it. It is often used by Virgil; but, if the several places be consulted, it will always be found with an *accusative* and *preposition*, expressed, or understood, as *magicas accingier artes*, or with an *accusative* and *dative*, as *accingere se praedae*, or, lastly, with an *ablative*, expressing the *instrument*, as *accingor ferro*. La Cerda, in his notes upon the place, seemed sensible of the objection, and therefore wrote, *Graeca locutio:* the common, but paltry, shift of learned critics, when they determine, at any rate, to support an ancient reading.

2. *Ardentes pugnas*, *burning battles*, sounds well enough to a modern ear; but I much doubt, if it would have passed in the times of Virgil. At least, I recollect no such expression in all his works; *ardens* being constantly joined to a word, denoting a *substance* of apparent *light*, *heat*, or *flame*, to which the allusion is easy, as *ardentes gladios*, *ardentes oculos*, *campos armis sublimibus ardentes*, and, by an easy metaphor, *ardentes hostes*; but no where, that I can find, to so *abstract* a notion, as that of *fight*. It seems to be to avoid this difficulty, that some have chosen to read *ardentis*, in the *genitive*, which yet Servius rejects as of no authority.

3. But the most glaring note of illegitimacy is in the line,

Tithoni primâ quot abest ab origine Caesar.

It has puzzled all the commentators from old Servius

temptation of disclosing thus much of one of the noblest fictions of antiquity; and the rather,

down to the learned Mr. Martyn, to give any tolerable account of the poet's choice of *Tithonus*, from whom to derive the ancestry of Augustus, rather than *Anchises*, or *Assaracus*, who were not only more famous, but in the *direct* line. The pretences of any, or all of them, are too frivolous to make it necessary to spend a thought about them. The instance stands single in antiquity; much less is there any thing like it to be found in the Augustan poets.

II. But the *phraseology* of these lines is the least of my objection. Were it ever so accurate, there is, besides, on the first view, a manifest absurdity in the *subject-matter* of them. For would any writer, of but common skill in the art of composition, close a long and elaborate allegory, the principal grace of which consists in its very mystery, with a cold and formal explanation of it? or would he pay so poor a compliment to his patron, as to suppose his sagacity wanted the assistance of this additional triplet to lead him into the true meaning? Nothing can be more abhorrent from the usual address and artifice of Virgil's manner. Or,

III. Were the *subject-matter* itself passable, yet, how, in defiance of all the laws of *disposition*, came it to be *forced* in here? Let the reader turn to the passage, and he will soon perceive, that this could never be the *place* for it. The allegory being concluded, the poet returns to his subject, which is proposed in the six following lines:

Interea Dryadum sylvas, saltusque sequamur
Intactos, tua, Maecenas, haud mollia jussa;

as the propriety of allegoric composition, which made the distinguished pride of ancient poetry,

Te sine nil altum mens incohat: en age segnes
Rumpe moras: vocat ingenti clamore Cithaeron,
Taygetique canes, domitrixque Epidaurus equorum,
Et vox assensu nemorum ingeminata remugit.

Would now any one expect, that the poet, after having conducted the reader, thus respectfully, to the very threshold of his subject, should immediately run away again to the point from which he had set out, and this on so needless an errand, as the letting him into the secret of his allegory?

But this inserted triplet agrees as ill with what *follows*, as with what *precedes* it. For how abrupt is the transition, and unlike the delicate connexion, so studiously contrived by the Augustan poets, from

Tithoni primâ quot abest ab origine Caesar,

to

Seu quis Olympiacae miratus praemia palmae, &c.

When, omit but these interpolated lines, and see how gracefully, and by how natural a succession of ideas, the poet slides into the main of his subject:

Intereà Dryadum sylvas saltusque sequamur
Intactos—
Te sine nil—
Rumpe moras: vocat ingenti clamore Cithaeron
Tagetique canes, domitrixque Epidaurus EQUORUM,
Et vox assensu nemorum ingeminata REMUGIT.
Seu quis Olympiacae miratus praemia palmae
Pascit EQUOS; *seu quis fortes ad aratra* JUVENCOS.

On the whole, I have not the least doubt, that the lines before us are the spurious offspring of some *later*

seems

ſeems but little known or attended to by the *modern* profeſſors of this fine art.

17. NIL ORITURUM ALIAS, NIL ORTUM TALE FATENTES.] *Il n'eſt impoſſible*, ſays M. DE BALZAC, in that puffed, declamatory rhapſody, entitled, LE PRINCE, *de reſiſter au mouvement*

poet; if indeed the writer of them deſerve that name; for, whoever he was, he is ſo far from partaking of the original ſpirit of Virgil, that at moſt he appears to have been but a ſervile and paltry mimic of Ovid; from the opening of whoſe Metamorphoſes the deſign was clearly taken. The turn of the thought is evidently the ſame in both, and even the *expreſſion*. *Mutatas dicere formas* is echoed by *ardentes dicere pugnas: dicere fert animus*, is, by an affected improvement, *accingar dicere:* and *Tithoni primâ ab origine* is almoſt literally the ſame as *primâque ab origine mundi*. For the *inſertion* of theſe lines in this place, I leave it to the curious to conjecture of it as they may; but in the mean time, muſt eſteem the office of the true *critic* to be ſo far reſembling that of the *poet* himſelf, as, within ſome proper limitations, to juſtify the *honeſt* liberty here taken.

Cum tabulis animum cenſoris ſumet honeſti;
Audebit quaecunque parum ſplendoris habebunt
Et ſine pondere erunt, et honore indigna feruntur,
VERBA MOVERE LOCO; QUAMVIS INVITA RECEDANT,
ET VERSENTUR ADHUC INTRA PENETRALIA VESTAE. [2 Ep. ii. 110.

interieur,

interieur, qui me pousse. Je ne sçaurois m'empecher de parler du ROY, *et de sa vertu; de crier à tous les princes, que c'est l'exemple, qu'ils doivent suivre;* DE DEMANDER A TOUS LES PEUPLES, ET A TOUS LES AGES, S'ILS ONT JAMAIS RIEN VEU DE SEMBLABLE. This was spoken of a king of France, who, it will be owned, had his virtues. But they were the virtues of the *man*, and not of the *prince*. This, however, was a distinction, which the eloquent encomiast was not aware of, or, to speak more truly, his business required him to overlook. For the whole elogy is worth perusing, as it affords a striking proof of the uniform genius of flattery, which, alike under all circumstances, and indifferent to all characters, can hold the same language of the weakest, as the ablest of princes, of LOUIS LE JUSTE, and CAESAR OCTAVIANUS AUGUSTUS.

23. SIC FAUTOR VETERUM, &c. to line 28.] The folly, here satirized, is common enough in all countries, and extends to all arts. It was just the same preposterous affectation of venerating antiquity, which put the connoisseurs in *painting*, under the emperors, on crying up the simple and rude sketches of AGLAOPHON and POLYGNOTUS, above the exquisite and finished pictures of PARRHASIUS and ZEUXIS. The account is given by Quinctilian, who, in his censure

censure of this absurdity, points to the undoubted source of it. His words are these: "Primi quorum quidem opera non vetustatis "modò gratiâ visenda sunt, clari pictores fuisse "dicuntur Polygnotus et Aglaophon; quorum "simplex color tam sui studiosos adhuc habet, "ut illa propè rudia ac velut futurae mox artis "primordia, maximis, qui post eos extiterunt, "auctoribus praeferantur, PROPRIO QUODAM "INTELLIGENDI (ut mea fert opinio) AMBITU." [L. xii. c. 10.] The lover of painting must be the more surprized at this strange *preference*, when he is told, that Aglaophon, at least, had the use of only *one single colour*; whereas Parrhasius and Zeuxis, who are amongst the *maximi auctores*, here glanced at, not only employed *different colours*, but were exceedingly eminent, the one of them for *correct drawing, and the delicacy of his outline*; the *other*, for his *invention* of that great secret of the *chiaro oscuro*. "Post Zeuxis et Parrhasius: quorum prior "LUMINUM UMBRARUMQUE INVENISSE RATIONEM, secundus, EXAMINASSE SUBTILIUS "LINEAS DICITUR." [Ibid.]

28. SI, QUIA GRAIORUM SUNT ANTIQUISSIMA QUAEQUE SCRIPTA vel OPTIMA, &c.] The common interpretation of this place supposes the poet to admit *the most ancient of the Greek*

Greek writings to be the best. Which were even contrary to all experience and common ſenſe, and is directly confuted by the hiſtory of the Greek learning. What he allows is, the *ſuperiority* of the oldeſt Greek writings *extant*; which is a very different thing. The turn of his argument confines us to this ſenſe. For he would ſhew the folly of concluding the ſame of the *old Roman* writers, on their *firſt* rude attempts to copy the finiſhed models of Greece, as of the *old Greek writers* themſelves, who were furniſhed with the means of producing thoſe *models* by long diſcipline and cultivation. This appears, certainly, from what follows:

Venimus ad ſummum fortunae: pingimus atque
Pſallimus et luctamur Achivis doctius unctis.

The deſign of which hath been entirely overlooked. For it hath been taken only for a *general expreſſion* of falſehood and abſurdity, of juſt the ſame import as the proverbial line,

Nil intra eſt oleâ, nil extra eſt in nuce duri.

Whereas it was *deſignedly* pitched upon to convey a *particular illuſtration* of the very abſurdity in queſtion, and to ſhew the maintainers of it, from the nature of things, how ſenſeleſs their poſition was. It is to this purpoſe: "As well "it may be pretended, that we *Romans* ſurpaſs "the *Greeks* in the arts of *painting, muſic, and*

"the

" *the exercises of the palaestra*, which yet it is
" confessed we do not, as that our *old* writers
" surpass the *modern*. The absurdity, in either
" case, is the same. For, as the Greeks, who
" had long devoted themselves, with great and
" continued application, to the practice of these
" arts (which is the force of the epithet UNCTI,
" here given them) must, for that reason, carry
" the prize from the Romans, who have taken
" very little pains about them; so, the modern
" Romans, who have for a long time been
" studying the *arts of poetry and composition*, must
" needs excel the old Ròman writers, who had
" little or no acquaintance with those arts, and
" had been trained, by no previous discipline,
" to the exercise of them."

The conciseness of the expression made it necessary to open the poet's sense at large. We now see that his intention, in these two lines, was to expose, in the way of *argumentative illustration*, the ground of that absurdity, which the preceding verses had represented as, at first sight, so shocking to *common sense*.

33. UNCTIS.] This is by no means a general, unmeaning epithet: but is beautifully chosen to express the unwearied *assiduity* of the Greek artists. For, the practice of *anointing* being essential to their agonistic trials, the poet

 elegantly

elegantly puts the attending *circumſtance* for the *thing* itſelf. And ſo, in ſpeaking of them, as UNCTI, he does the ſame, as if he had called them "the induſtrious, or *exerciſing* Greeks;" which was the very idea his argument required him to ſuggeſt to us.

43.—HONESTE.] Expreſſing the *credit* ſuch a piece was held in, as had the fortune to be ranked *inter veteres*, agreeably to what he ſaid above—PERFECTOS *vetereſque*, line 37—and—*vetus atque* PROBUS, line 39: which affords a freſh preſumption in favour of Dr. Bentley's conjecture on line 41, where, inſtead of *veteres poetas*, he would read,

Inter quos referendus erit? vetereſne PROBOSQUE,
An quos, &c.

54. ADEO SANCTUM EST VETUS OMNE POEMA.] The reader is not to ſuppoſe, that Horace, in this ridicule of the fooliſh adorers of antiquity, intended any contempt of the old Roman poets; who, as the old writers in every country, abound in ſtrong ſenſe, vigorous expreſſion, and the trueſt repreſentation of life and manners. His quarrel is only with the critic:

Qui redit in faſtos et virtutem aeſtimat annis.

An affectation, which for its *folly*, if it had not

too

too apparently ſprung from a worſe principle, deſerved to be laughed at.

For the reſt, he every where diſcovers a candid and juſt eſteem of their earlier writers; as may be ſeen from many places in this very epiſtle; but more eſpecially from that ſevere cenſure in 1 S. x. 17. (which hath more of acrimony in it than he uſually allows to his ſatire) when, in ſpeaking of the writers of the old comedy, he adds,

Quos neque pulcher
Hermogenes unquam legit, neque ſimius iſte
Nil praeter Calvum et doctus cantare Catullum.

With all his zeal for correct writing, he was not, we ſee, of the humour of that delicate ſort, who are for burning their old poets; and, to be well with women and court-critics, confine their reading and admiration to the innocent ſing-ſong of ſome ſoft and faſhionable rhymer, whoſe utter inſipidity is a thouſand times more inſufferable than any barbariſm.

56. Pacuvius docti famam senis, Accius alti.] The epithet *doctus*, here applied to the tragic poet, *Pacuvius*, is, I believe, ſometimes miſunderſtood, though the oppoſition to *altus* clearly determines the ſenſe. For, as this laſt word expreſſes the *ſublime* of ſentiment and expreſſion, which comes from *nature*, ſo the former word muſt needs be interpreted of that

exactneſs

exactneſs in both, or at leaſt of that *ſkill* in the conduct of the ſcene (the proper *learning* of a dramatic poet) which is the reſult of *art*.

The Latin word *doctus* is indeed ſomewhat ambiguous: but we are chiefly miſled by the Engliſh word, *learned*, by which we tranſlate it, and by which, in general uſe, is meant, rather extenſive reading, and what we call *erudition*, than a profound ſkill in the rules and principles of any art. But this laſt is frequently the ſenſe of the Latin term *doctus*, as we may ſee from its application, in the beſt claſſic writers, to other, beſides the literary profeſſions. Thus, to omit other inſtances, we find it applied very often in Horace himſelf. It is applied to a *ſinging-girl*—*doctae* pſallere Chiae—in one of his Odes, l. iv. 13. It is applied to ſeveral *mechanic arts* in this epiſtle—“ *doctius* “ Achivis pingimus atque pſallimus et luctamur:” It is even applied, *abſolutely*, to the player Roſcius—*doctus* Roſcius, in line 82, where his ſkill in *acting* could only be intended by it. It is, alſo, in this ſenſe, that he calls his imitator, *doctus*, i. e. ſkilled and knowing in his art, A. P. line 319. Nay, it is preciſely in this ſenſe that Quinctilian uſes the word, when he characterizes this very Pacuvius—*Pacuvium videri* doctiorem, *qui eſſe docti affectant, volunt* [l. x. c. 1.] i. e. *they, who affect to be thought know-*

ing

ing in the rules of dramatic writing, give this praise to Pacuvius. The expression is so put, as if Quinctilian intended a censure of these critics; because this pretence to dramatic art, and the strict imitation of the Greek poets, was grown, in his time, and long before it, into a degree of pedantry and *affectation*; no other merit, but this of *docti*, being of any significancy, in their account. There is no reason to think that Quinctilian meant to insinuate the poet's want of this merit, or his own contempt of it: though he might think, and with reason, that too much stress had been laid upon it by some men.

It is in the same manner that one of our own poets has been characterized; and the application of this term to him will shew the force of it, still more clearly.

In Mr. Pope's fine imitation of this epistle, are these lines—

In all debates, where critics bear a part,
Not one but nods and talks of Jonson's *art*—

One sees, then, how Mr. Pope understood the *docti*, of Horace. But our Milton applies the word *learned* itself, and in the Latin sense of it, to Jonson—

When Jonson's *learned* sock is on—

For what is this *learning?* Indisputably, his *dramatic learning*, his skill in the scene, and his

 observance

obſervance of the ancient rules and practice. For, though Jonſon was indeed *learned*, in every ſenſe; it is the learning of his profeſſion, as a comic artiſt, for which he is here celebrated.

The Latin ſubſtantive, *doctrina*, is uſed with the ſame latitude, as the adjective, *doctus*. It ſometimes ſignifies the *peculiar ſort* of learning, under conſideration; though ſometimes again it ſignifies *learning*, or erudition, at large. It is uſed in the former ſenſe by Cicero, when he obſerves of the ſatires of Lucilius, that they were remarkable for their wit and pleaſantry, not for their *learning—doctrina* mediocris. So that there is no contradiction in this judgment, as is commonly thought, to that of Quinctilian, who declares roundly—*eruditio* in eo mira— For, though *doctrina* and *eruditio* be ſometimes convertible terms, they are not ſo here. The *learning* Cicero ſpeaks of in Lucilius, as being but *moderate*, is his learning, or ſkill, in the art of writing and compoſition.—That this was the whole purport of Cicero's obſervation, any one may ſee by turning to the place where it occurs, in the proeme to his firſt book DE FINIBUS.

59. VINCERE CAECILIUS GRAVITATE, TERENTIUS ARTE.] It ſhould be obſerved, that the

the judgment, here passed [from line 55 to 60] on the most celebrated Roman writers, being only a representation of the *popular* opinion, not of the poet's *own*, the commendations given to them are deserved, or otherwise, just as it chances.

Interdum vulgus rectum videt, est ubi peccat.

To give an instance of this in the line before us.

A critic of unquestioned authority acquaints us, wherein the *real distinct merit* of these two dramatic writers consists. "In ARGUMENTIS, "Caecilius palmam poscit; in ETHESIN, TE-"RENTIUS." [Varro.] Now by *gravitate*, as applied to Caecilius, we may properly enough understand the *grave and affecting cast* of his comedy; which is farther confirmed by what the same critic elsewhere observes of him: "PATHE "Trabea, Attilius, et CAECILIUS facile move-"runt." But Terence's characteristic of *painting the manners*, which is, plainly, the right interpretation of Varro's ETHESIN, is not so significantly expressed by the attribute *arte*, here given to him. The word indeed is of large and general import, and may admit of various senses; but, being here applied to a *dramatic* writer, it most naturally and properly denotes the *peculiar* art of his profession, that is, *the artificial contexture of the plot*. And this, I doubt not, was the very praiſe, the town-critics of Horace's time intended to beſtow on this poet. The matter is eaſily explained.

The ſimplicity, and exact unity of the plots in the Greek comedies would be, of courſe, uninteresting to a people, not thoroughly inſtructed in the genuine beauties of the drama. They had too thin a contexture to ſatisfy the groſs and lumpiſh taſte of a Roman auditory. The Latin poets, therefore, bethought themſelves of combining two ſtories into one. And this, which is what we call the *double plot*, affording the opportunity of more incidents, and a greater variety of *action*, was perfectly ſuited to their apprehenſions. But, of all the Latin comedians, *Terence* appears to have practiſed this ſecret moſt aſſiduouſly: at leaſt, as may be concluded from what remains of them. *Plautus* hath very frequently *ſingle plots*, which he was enabled to ſupport by, what was natural to him, a force of buffoon pleaſantry. *Terence*, whoſe genius lay another way, or whoſe taſte was abhorrent from ſuch ribaldry, had recourſe to the other expedient of *double plots*. And this, I ſuppoſe, is what gained him the popular reputation of being the moſt *artificial* writer for the ſtage. The HECYRA is the only one of his comedies, of the true ancient caſt. And we know how it came off in the repreſentation. That ill-ſucceſs, and the ſimplicity

city of its conduct have continued to draw upon it the ſame unfavourable treatment from the critics, to this day; who conſtantly ſpeak of it, as much inferior to the reſt; whereas, for the genuine beauty of dramatic deſign, and the obſervance, after the ancient Greek manner, of the nice dependency and coherence of the *fable* throughout, it is, indiſputably, to every reader of true taſte, the moſt maſterly and exquiſite of the whole collection.

63. INTERDUM VULGUS RECTUM VIDET: EST UBI PECCAT.] The capricious levity of *popular opinion* hath been noted even to a proverb. And yet it is this, which, after all, *fixes* the fate of authors. This ſeemingly odd phænomenon I would thus account for.

What is uſually complimented with the high and reverend appellation of *public judgment* is, in any ſingle inſtance, but the repetition or echo, for the moſt part eagerly catched, and ſtrongly reverberated on all ſides, of a few leading voices, which have happened to gain the confidence, and ſo direct the *cry*, of the public. But (as, in fact, it too often falls out) this prerogative of the *few* may be abuſed to the prejudice of the *many*. The partialities of friendſhip, the faſhionableneſs of the writer, his compliance with the reigning taſte, the lucky concurrence of time and opportunity, the cabal of a party, nay, the very freaks of whim and caprice; theſe, or any of them, as occaſion ſerves, can ſupport the dulleſt, as the oppoſite diſadvantages can depreſs the nobleſt, performance; and give a currency or neglect to *either*, far beyond what the genuine character of each demands. Hence the *public voice*, which is but the aggregate of theſe corrupt judgments, infinitely multiplied, is, with the wiſe, at ſuch a juncture, deſervedly of little eſteem. Yet, in a ſucceſſion of ſuch *judgments*, delivered at different times, and by different ſets or juntos of theſe ſovereign arbiters of the fate of authors, the public opinion naturally gets clear of theſe accidental corruptions. Every freſh ſucceſſion ſhakes off ſome; till, by degrees, the work is ſeen in its proper form, unſupported of every other recommendation, than what its native inherent excellence beſtows upon it. Then, and not till then, *the voice of the people* becomes ſacred; after which it ſoon advances into *divinity*, before which all ages muſt fall down and worſhip. For now reaſon alone, without her corrupt aſſeſſors, takes the chair. And her ſentence, when once promulgated, and authorized by the general voice, fixes the unalterable doom of authors. ΟΛΩΣ ΚΑΛΑ ΝΟΜΙΖΕ ΥΨΗ ΚΑΙ ΑΛΗΘΙΝΑ, ΤΑ ΔΙΑΠΑΝΤΟΣ ΑΡΕΣΚΟΝΤΑ ΚΑΙ ΠΑΣΙΝ. [Longinus, § vii.]

§ vii.] And the reaſon follows, agreeably to the account here given. Ὅταν γὰρ τοῖς ἀπὸ διαφόρων ΕΠΙΤΗΔΕΥΜΑΤΩΝ, ΒΙΩΝ, ΖΗΛΩΝ, ΗΛΙΚΙΩΝ, λόγων, ἕν τι καὶ ταὐτὸν ἅμα περὶ τῶν αὐτῶν ἅπασι δοκῇ, τόθ' ἡ ἐξ ἀσυμφώνων ὡς κρίσις καὶ συγκατάθεσις τὴν ἐπὶ τῷ θαυμαζομένῳ ΠΙΣΤΙΝ ΙΣΧΥΡΑΝ ΛΑΜΒΑΝΕΙ ΚΑΙ ΑΝΑΜΦΙΛΕΚΤΟΝ. [Ibid.]

This is the true account of *popular fame*, which, while it well explains the ground of the poet's aphoriſm, ſuggeſts an obvious remark, but very mortifying to every candidate of literary glory. It is, that, whether he ſucceeds in his endeavours after public applauſe, or not, *fame* is equally out of his reach, and, as the moral poet teaches, *a thing beyond him, before his death*, on either ſuppoſition. For at the very time, that this bewitching muſic is ſounding in his ears, he can never be ſure, if, inſtead of the divine conſentient harmony of a juſt praiſe, it be not only the diſcordant din and clamour of ignorance or prepoſſeſſion.

If there be any exception to this melancholy truth, it muſt be in the caſe of ſome uncommon genius, whoſe ſuperior power breaks through all impediments in his road to fame, and forces applauſe even from thoſe very prejudices, that would obſtruct his career to it.

 It

It was the rare felicity of the poet, just mentioned, to receive, in his life-time, this sure and pleasing augury of immortality.

.81. INGENIIS NON ILLE FAVET, &c.] MALHERBE was to the French, pretty much what HORACE had been to the Latin, poetry. These great writers had, each of them, rescued the lyric muse of their country out of the rude, ungracious hands of their old poets. And, as their talents of a *good ear*, *elegant judgment*, and *correct expression*, were the same, they presented her to the public in all the air and grace, and yet *severity*, of beauty, of which her form was susceptible. Their merits and pretensions being thus far resembling, the reader may not be incurious to know the fate and fortune of *each*. *Horace* hath very frankly told us, what befel himself from the malevolent and low passions of his countrymen. *Malherbe* did not come off, with the wits and critics of his time, much better; as we learn from a learned person, who hath very warmly recommended his writings to the public. Speaking of the envy, which pursued him in his *prose-works*; but, says he, "comme "il faisoit une particuliere profession de la *poesie*, "c'est en cette qualité qu'il a de plus severes "censeurs, et receu des injustices plus signalées. "Mais il me semble que je fermerai la bouche

"à ceux,

" à ceux, qui le blament, quand je leur aurai " monſtré, que ſa façon d'eſcrire eſt excellente, " quoiqu'elle s'eloigne un peu de celle des NOS " ANCIENS POETES, QU'ILS LOUENT PLUSTOT " PAR UN DEGOUST DES CHOSES PRESENTES, " QUE PAR LES SENTIMENTS D'UNE VERI- " TABLE ESTIME." [DISC. DE M. GODEAU SUR LES OEUVRES DE M. MALHERBE.]

97. SUSPENDIT MENTEM VULTUMQUE.] The expreſſion hath great elegance, and is not liable to the imputation of *harſh, or improper conſtruction*. For *ſuſpendit* is not taken, with regard either to *mentem* or *vultum*, in its *literal*, but *figurative*, ſignification; and, thus, it becomes, in one and the *ſame* ſenſe, applicable to *both*.

Otherwiſe, this way of coupling *two ſubſtantives* to a *verb*, which does not, in ſtrict grammatical uſage, *govern* both; or, if it doth, muſt needs be conſtrued in different ſenſes; hath given juſt offence to the beſt critics.

Mr. Pope cenſures a paſſage of this kind, in the *Iliad*, with ſeverity; and thinks *the taſte of the antients was, in general, too good for theſe fooleries* [*f*].

Mr. Addiſon is perfectly of the ſame mind, as appears from his criticiſm on that line in

[*f*] B. ix. 641.

Ovid,

Ovid, *Consiliis, non curribus utere nostris.* "This "way of joining, says he, two such different "ideas as chariot and counsel to the same verb, "is mightily used by *Ovid*; but is a very low "kind of wit, and has always in it a mixture of "*pun*; because the verb must be taken in a dif-"ferent sense, when it is joined with one of the "things, from what it has in conjunction with "the other. Thus, in the end of this story, he "tells you, that Jupiter flung a thunberbolt at "Phaëton: *pariterque animaque rotisque expulit* "*aurigam:* where he makes a forced piece of "*Latin (animâ expulit aurigam)* that he may "couple the soul and the wheels to the same "verb [g]."

These, the reader will think, are pretty good authorities. For, in matters of *taste*, I know of none, that more deserve to be regarded. The *mere verbal critic*, one would think, should be cautious, how he opposed himself to them. And yet a very learned Dutchman, who has taken great pains in *elucidating* an old Greek love-story, which, with its more passionate admirers, may, perhaps, pass for the MARIANNE of antiquity, hath not scrupled to censure this decision of theirs very sharply [h].

[g] *Notes on the story of Phaëton*, line 23.

[h] JACOBI PHILIPPI D'ORVILLE *Animadversiones in* CHARIT. APHROD. lib. iv. c. 4.

Having

Having tranſcribed the cenſure of Mr. Pope, who, indeed ſomewhat too haſtily, ſuſpects the line in Homer for an interpolation, our critic faſtens upon him directly. EN COR ZENODOTI, EN JECUR CRATETIS! But foul language and fair criticiſm are different things; and what he offers of the *latter* rather accounts for than juſtifies the *former*. All he ſays on the ſubject, is in the good old way of *authorities*, which he diligently rakes together out of every corner of Greek and Roman antiquity. From all theſe he concludes, as he thinks, irreſiſtibly, not that the paſſage in queſtion *might* be *genuine* (for *that* few would diſpute with him) but that the kind of expreſſion itſelf is a *real beauty*. *Bona elocutio eſt: honeſta figura.* Though, to the praiſe of his diſcretion be it remembered, he does not even venture on this aſſertion, without his uſual ſupport of *precedent*. And, for want of a better, he takes up with old *Servius*. For ſo, it ſeems, this grammarian hath declared himſelf, with reſpect to ſome expreſſions of the ſame kind in *Virgil*.

But let him make the beſt of his authorities. And, when he has done that, I ſhall take the liberty to aſſure him, that the perſons, he contends againſt, do not think themſelves in the leaſt concerned with them. For, though he believes it an undeniable maxim, *Critici non eſſe inquirere, utrum recte auctor quid ſcripſerit, ſed an omnino*

omnino sic scripserit [*i*]: yet, in the case before us, he must not be surprized, if others do not so conceive of it.

Indeed, where the critic would defend the *authenticity* of a word or expression, the way of *precedent* is, doubtless, the very best, that common sense allows to be taken. For the evidence of *fact*, at once, bears down all suspicion of *corruption* or *interpolation*. Again; if the *elegance* of single words (or of entire phrases, where the suspicion turns on the *oddity or uncommoness of the construction*, only) be the matter in dispute, full and precise authorities must decide it. For *elegance*, here, means nothing else but the practice of the best writers. And thus far I would join issue with the learned censurer; and should think he did well in prescribing this rule to himself in the correction of *approved ancient authors*.

But what have these cases to do with the point in question? The objection is made, not to *words*, which alone are capable of being justified by authority, but to *things*, which must ever be what they are, in spite of it. This mode of writing is shewn to be abundantly defective, for reasons taken from *the nature of our ideas, and the end and genius of the nobler forms of composition*. And what is it to tell us, that great writers have overlooked or neglected them?

[*i*] Ibid. vol. ii. p. 325.

1. In

1. In our cuſtomary train of *thinking*, the mind is carried along, *in ſucceſſion*, from *one* clear and diſtinct idea to *another*. Or, if the attention be *at once* employed on *two ſenſes*, there is ever ſuch a cloſe and near analogy betwixt them, that the perceptive faculty, eaſily, and almoſt inſtantaneouſly, paſſing from the one to the other, is not divided in its regards betwixt them, but even ſeems to itſelf to conſider them, as *one*: as is the caſe with *metaphor*; and, univerſally, with all the juſt forms of *alluſion*. The union between the *literal* and *figurative* ſenſe is ſo ſtrict, that they run together in the imagination; and the effect of the *figure* is only to let in freſh light and luſtre on the *literal* meaning. But now, when *two different*, *unconnected ideas* are obtruded at the ſame time upon us, the mind ſuffers a kind of violence and diſtraction, and is thereby put out of that natural ſtate, in which it ſo much delights. To take the learned writer's inſtance from Polybius: ΕΛΠΙΔΑ ϗ ΧΕΙΡΑ ΠΡΟΣΛΑΜΒΑΝΕΙΝ. How different is the idea of *collecting forces*, and of that *act* of the mind, which we call *taking courage*! Theſe two *perceptions* are not only diſtinct from each other, but totally unconnected by any *natural* bond of relationſhip betwixt them. And yet the word ΠΡΟΣΛΑΜΒΑΝΕΙΝ muſt be ſeen in this double

view,

view, before we can take the full meaning of the hiſtorian.

2. This conjunction of *unrelated* ideas, by the means of a *common term*, agrees as ill to the *end and genius of the writer's compoſition*, as *the natural bent and conſtitution of the mind*. For the queſtion is only about the *greater poetry*, which addreſſes itſelf to the PASSIONS, or IMAGINATION. And, in either caſe, this play of words, which Mr. Pope condemns, muſt be highly out of ſeaſon.

When we are neceſſitated, as it were, to look different ways, and actually to contemplate two unconnected ſignifications of the ſame word, before we can thoroughly comprehend its purpoſe; the mind is more amuſed by this fanciful conjunction of ideas, than is conſiſtent with the artleſs, undeſigning ſimplicity of *paſſion*. It diſturbs and interrupts the flow of *affection*, by preſenting this diſparted image to the *fancy*. Again; where *fancy* itſelf is ſolely addreſſed, as in the *nobler deſcriptive ſpecies*, this arbitrary aſſemblage of ideas is not leſs improper. For the poet's buſineſs is now, to aſtoniſh or entertain the mind with a ſucceſſion of *great* or *beautiful* images. And the intervention of this juggler's trick diverts the thought from contemplating its proper ſcenery. We ſhould be admiring ſome glorious repreſentation of *nature*, and are ſtopped, on a ſudden, to obſerve the writer's *art*,

whoſe

whose ingenuity can fetch, out of one word, two such foreign and discrepant meanings.

In the lighter forms of poetry indeed, and more especially in the *burlesque epic*, this affectation has its *place*; as in that line of Mr. Pope, quoted by this critic;

Sometimes counsel takes, *and sometimes tea.*

For, 1. The writer's intention is here, not to *affect the passions*, or *transport the fancy*, but solely to *divert and amuse*. And to such *end* this species of trifling is very apposite. 2. The *manner*, which the burlesque epic takes to divert, is by confounding *great things with small*. A *mode of speech* then, which favours such *confusion*, is directly to its purpose. 3. This poem is, by its nature, *satirical*, and, like the *old comedy*, delights in exposing the faults and vices of *composition*. So that the *expression* is here properly employed (and this was, perhaps, the *first* view of the writer) to ridicule the use of it in *grave works*. If M. *D'Orville* then could seriously design to confute Mr. Pope's criticism by his own practice in that line of the *Rape of the Lock*, he has only shewn, that he does not, in the least, comprehend the real genius of this poem. But to return:

There is, as appears to me, but one case, in which this *double sense* of words can be admitted in in the more ſolemn forms of poetry. It is, when, beſides the plain literal meaning, which the context demands, the mind is carried forward to ſome more illuſtrious and important object. We have an inſtance in the famous line of Virgil,

Attollens humeris famamque et fata nepotum.

But this is ſo far from contradicting, that it furthers the writer's proper intention. We are not called off from the *ſubject-matter* to the obſervation of a *conceit*, but to the admiration of *kindred* ſublime conceptions. For even here, it is to be obſerved, there is always required ſome previous dependency and relationſhip, though not extremely obvious, in the natures of the things themſelves, whereon to ground and juſtify the analogy. Otherwiſe, the intention of the *double ſenſe* is perfectly inexcuſable.

But the inſtance from Virgil, as we have ſeen it explained (and for the firſt time) by a great critic [*i*], is ſo curious, that I ſhall be allowed to enlarge a little upon it: and the rather, as Virgil's practice in this inſtance will let us into the true ſecret of conducting theſe *double ſenſes*.

The comment of *Servius* on this line is remarkable: " Hunc verſum notant critici, " quaſi ſuperfluè et inutiliter additum, nec con-

[*i*] D. L. vol. ii. p. 644.

" venientem *gravitati* ejus, namque eſt magis " *neotericus*." Mr. Addiſon conceived of it in the ſame manner, when he ſaid, " *This was* " *the only witty line in the Æneis*;" meaning ſuch a line as *Ovid* would have written. We ſee the opinion which theſe Critics entertained of the *double ſenſe*, in *general*, in the greater Poetry. They eſteemed it a wanton play of fancy, miſbecoming the dignity of the writer's work, and the gravity of his character. They took it, in ſhort, for a mere *modern* flouriſh, totally different from the pure unaffected manner of genuine antiquity. And thus far they unqueſtionably judged right. Their defect was in not ſeeing that the *uſe* of it, as here employed by the Poet, was an exception to the *general rule*. But to have ſeen this was not, perhaps, to be expected even from theſe Critics.

However, from this want of penetration aroſe a difficulty in determining whether to read, *Facta* or *Fata* Nepotum. And, as we now underſtand that *Servius* and his Critics were utter ſtrangers to Virgil's noble idea, it is no wonder they could not reſolve it. But the *latter* is the Poet's own word. He conſidered this ſhield of celeſtial make as a kind of Palladium, like the Ancile, which fell from Heaven, and uſed to be carried in proceſſion on the ſhoulders of the Salii. " Quid de ſcutis, ſays Lactantius, jam

" vetustate putridis dicam? Quæ cum portant,
" *Deos ipsos se gestare* HUMERIS SUIS *arbitran-*
" *tur.*" [Div. Inst. l. i. c. 21.]

Virgil, in a fine flight of imagination, alludes to this venerable ceremony, comparing, as it were, the shield of his Hero to the sacred ANCILE; and in conformity to the practice in that sacred procession represents his Hero in the priestly office of Religion,

Attollens HUMERO *famamque et* FATA *Nepotum.*

This idea then of the sacred shield, the guard and glory of Rome, and on which, in this advanced situation, depended the fame and fortune of his country, the poet, with extreme elegance and sublimity, transfers to the shield which guarded their great progenitor, while he was laying the first foundations of the Roman Empire.

But to return to the subject before us. What has been said of the impropriety of *double senses*, holds of *the construction of a single term in two senses*, even though its authorized usage may equally admit *both*. So that I cannot be of a mind with the learned critic's *wise men* [*k*]; *who acknowledge an extreme elegance in this form,*

[*k*] At inspiciamus porrò, quid alii, *quibus correctius sapit*, de hoc loquendi modo CENSUERINT. Agnoscunt enim, etc. p. 299.

when

when the governing verb equally corresponds to the two substantives. But when it properly can be applied but to *one* of them, and with some force and straining only to the *second*, as commonly happens with the application of *one verb to two substantives*, it then degenerates, as Mr. Addison observes, into a mere *quibble*, and is utterly incompatible with the graver forms of composition. And for this we have the concurrent authority of the *cordati* themselves, who readily admit, *duram admodum et καταχρηστικωτέραν fieri orationem, si verbum hoc ab alterutro abhorreat* [*l*]. Without softening matters, besides the former absurdity of *a second sense*, we are now indebted to a forced and barbarous construction for *any* second sense *at all*.

But surely this venerable bench of critics, to whom our censurer thinks fit to make his solemn appeal, were not aware of the imprudence of this concession. For why, if one may presume to ask, is the *latter* use of this *figure* condemned, but for reasons, which shew the manifest absurdity of the thing, however countenanced by authorities? And is not this the case of the *former*? Or, is the transgression of the standing rules of *good sense*, in the judgment of these *censors*, a more pardonable crime in a writer, than of *common usage or grammar*?

[*l*] Ibid.

After all, ſince he lays ſo great ſtreſs on his *authorities*, it may not be amiſs to conſider the proper force of them.

The form of ſpeaking under conſideration has been cenſured as a *trifling*, *affected witticiſm*. This *cenſure* he hopes entirely to elude, by ſhewing it was in uſe, more eſpecially among two ſorts of perſons, the leaſt likely to be infected with *wrong taſte*, the *oldeſt*, that is to ſay, the *ſimpleſt*; and the moſt *refined* writers. In ſhort, he thinks to ſtop all mouths, by alledging inſtances from *Homer* and *Virgil*.

But what if Homer and Virgil in the few examples of this kind to be met with in their writings have *erred?* And, which is more, what if that very *ſimplicity* on the one hand, and *refinement* on the other, which he builds ſo much upon, can be ſhewn to be the *natural* and almoſt neceſſary *occaſions* of their falling into ſuch *errors?* This, I am perſuaded, was the truth of the caſe. For,

1. In the *ſimpler ages of learning*, when, as yet, compoſition is not turned into an *art*, but every writer, eſpecially of vehement and impetuous genius, is contented to put down his *firſt thoughts*, and, for their *expreſſion*, takes up with the moſt obvious words and phraſes that preſent themſelves to him, this improper conſtruction will not be unfrequent. For the writer.

writer, who is not knowing enough to take offence at theſe niceties, having an immediate occaſion to expreſs *two things*, and finding *one word*, which, in common uſage, at leaſt with a little ſtraining, extends to *both*, he looks no further, but, as ſuſpecting no fault, employs it without ſcruple. And I am the more confirmed in this account, from obſerving, that ſometimes, where the governing *verb* cannot be made to bear this double ſenſe, and yet the meaning of the writer is clear enough from the context, the proper word is altogether omitted. Of this kind are ſeveral of the *modes of ſpeaking*, alledged by the writer as inſtances of the *double ſenſe*. As in that of Sophocles [*u*], where Electra, giving orders to Chryſothemis, about the diſpoſal of the *libations*, deſtined for the tomb of her father, delivers herſelf thus,

ΑΛΛ' ἢ ΠΝΟΑΙΣΙΝ, ἢ *βαθυσκαφεῖ* ΚΟΝΕΙ
ΚΡΥΨΟΝ νιν.

The writer's firſt intention was to look out for ſome ſuch *verb*, as would equally correſpond to πνοαῖς and κόνει· but this not occurring, he ſets down one, that only agrees to the laſt, and leaves the other to be underſtood, or ſupplied by the reader; as it eaſily might, the ſcope of the place neceſſarily directing him to it. It cannot

[*u*] Line 437.

be ſuppoſed, that Sophocles deſigned to ſay, κρύψον πνοαῖς. There is no affinity of *ſenſe* or *ſound* to lead him to ſuch conſtruction. Again; in that verſe of Homer [*n*],

"ΙΠΠΟΙ ἀερσίποδες, καὶ ποικίλα ΤΕΥΧΕ' ΕΚΕΙΤΟ,

the poet never meant to ſay ἵπποι ἔκειντο, but neglectingly left it thus, as truſting the nature of the thing would inſtruct the reader to ſupply ἕστασαν, or ſome ſuch word expreſſive of the *poſture* required.

Nay, writers of more exactneſs than theſe ſimple Greek poets have occaſionally overlooked ſuch inaccuracies: as Cicero [*o*], who, when more intent on his *argument* than *expreſſion*, lets fall this impropriety, *Nec vero* SUPRA TERRAM, *ſed etiam* IN INTIMIS EJUS TENEBRIS *plurimarum rerum* LATET *utilitas*. It is plain, the writer, conceiving *extat*, *patet*, or ſome ſuch word, to be neceſſarily ſuggeſted by the tenor of his ſentence, never troubled himſelf to go back to inſert it. Yet theſe are brought as examples of the *double application of ſingle words*. The truth is, they are examples of *indiligence* in the writers, and as ſuch, may ſhew us, how eaſily they might fall, for the ſame reaſon, into the impropriety of *double ſenſes*. In thoſe of this claſs

[*n*] Iliad, Γ. 327. [*o*] N. D. ii. 64.

then

then the impropriety, complained of, is the effect of mere *inattention or carelessness*.

2. On the other hand, when this negligent simplicity of *thinking and speaking* gives way to the utmost polish and refinement in *both*, we are then to expect it, for the contrary reason. For the more obvious and natural forms of writing being, now, grown common, are held insipid, and the public taste demands to be gratified by the seasoning of a more studied and artificial expression. It is not enough to *please*; the writer must find means to *strike* and *surprize*. And hence the *antithesis*, the *remote allusion*, and every other mode of *affected eloquence*. But of these the *first* that prevails, is the application of the *double sense*. For, the general use justifying it, it easily passes with the reader and writer too, for *natural* expression; and yet as splitting the attention suddenly, and at once, on two different views, carries with it all the novelty and surprize, that are wanted. When the public taste is not, yet, far gone in this refinement, and the writer hath himself the truest taste (which was VIRGIL's case), such affectations will not be very common; or, when they do occur, will, for the most part, be agreeably softened. As in the instance of *retroque pedem cum voce repressit*; where, by making *voce* immediately dependent on the *preposition*, and re-

 motely

motely on the *verb*, he ſoftens the harſhneſs of the expreſſion, which ſeems much more tolerable in this form, than if he had put it, *pedem vocemque repreſſit*. So again in the line,

> *Crudeles aras trajectaque pectora ferro*
> *Nudavit,*

the incongruity of *the two ſenſes* in *nudavit*, is the leſs perceived from its *metaphorical application* to *one* of them.

But the deſire of *pleaſing continually*, which, in the ciruinſtances ſuppoſed, inſenſibly grows into a *habit*, muſt, of neceſſity, betray writers of leſs taſte and exactneſs into the frequent commiſſion of this fault. Which, as Mr. Addiſon takes notice, was remarkably the caſe with OVID.

The purpoſe of all this is to ſhew, that the uſe of this *form of ſpeaking* aroſe from *negligence*, or *affectation*, never from *judgment*. And ſuch being the obvious, and, it is preſumed, true account of the matter, the learned *animadvertor* on CHARITON is left, as I ſaid, to make the beſt of his *authorities*; or, even to enlarge his liſt of them with the *centuries* [*o*] of his good friends, at his leiſure. For till he can tell us of a writer, who, neither in his *careleſs* nor *ambitious* humours, is capable of this folly, his accumulated citations, were they more to his pur-

[*o*] Pag. 397.

poſe

pose than many of them are, will do him little service. Unless, perhaps, we are to give up common sense to authority, and pride ourselves on mimicking the very defects of our *betters*. And even here he need not be at a loss for *precedents*. For so the disciples of Plato, we are told, in former times, affected to be *round-shoulder'd*, in compliment to their master; and Aristotle's worshipers, because of a natural impediment in this philosopher's speech, thought it to their credit to turn *stammerers*. And without doubt, while this fashion prevailed, there were critics, who found out a *je ne sçai quoi* in the *air* of the one party, and in the *eloquence* of the other.

97. SUSPENDIT PICTA VULTUM MENTEMQUE TABELLA.] Horace judiciously describes *painting* by that peculiar circumstance, which does most honour to this fine art. It is, that, in the hands of a master, it attaches, not the *eyes* only, but the very *soul*, to its representation of the *human affections and manners*. For it is in contemplating *subjects* of this kind, that the mind, with a fond and eager attention, *hangs* on the picture. Other imitations may *please*, but this warms and transports with *passion*. And, because whatever addresses itself immediately to the *eye* affects us most, hence it is, that painting, so employed, becomes more efficacious to

expreſs

expreſs the *manners* and imprint *characters*, than poetry itſelf: or rather, hath the advantages of the beſt and uſefulleſt ſpecies of poetry, the *dramatic*, when enforced by juſt action on the ſtage.

Quinctilian gives it the like preference to *oratory*. Speaking of the uſe of *action* in an orator, he obſerves, "Is [geſtus] quantum ha-"beat in oratore, momenti; ſatis vel ex eo "patet, quod pleraque, etiam citra verba, ſigni-"ficat. Quippe non manus ſolum, ſed nutus "etiam declarant noſtram voluntatem, et in "mutis pro ſermone ſunt: et ſalutatio fre-"quenter ſine voce intelligitur atque afficit, et "ex ingreſſu vultuque perſpicitur habitus ani-"morum: et animantium quoque, ſermone ca-"rentium, ira, laetitia, adulatio, et oculis et "quibuſdam aliis corporis ſignis deprehenditur. "Nec mirum, ſi iſta, quae tamen aliquo ſunt "poſita motu, tantum in animis valent: quum "*pictura, tacens opus, et habitûs ſemper ejuſdem, ſic* "*intimos penetret affectus, ut ipſam vim dicendi* "*nonnunquam ſuperare videatur* [*p*]."

We ſee then of what importance it is, ſince *affections* of every kind are equally within his power, that the painter apply himſelf to excite only *thoſe*, which are ſubſervient to good morals. An importance, of which Ariſtotle himſelf (who

[*p*] Inst. Orat. xi. 3.

was

was no enthusiast in the fine arts) was so sensible, that he gives it in charge, amongst other political instructions, to the governors of youth, "that they allow them to see no other pictures, "than such as have this moral aim and tendency; of which kind were more especially "those of POLYGNOTUS." [POLIT. lib. viii. c. 5.]

For the manner, in which this moral efficacy of picture is brought about, we find it agreeably explained in that conversation of *Socrates* with *Parrhasius* in the *Memorabilia* of Xenophon. The whole may be worth considering.

"PAINTING, said Socrates, one day, in a "conversation with the painter Parrhasius, is, I "think, the resemblance or imitation of sensible objects. For you represent in colours, "bodies of all sorts, *hollow and projecting*, *bright and obscure*, *hard and soft*, *old and new*."—"We "do."—"And, when you would draw beautiful "pourtraits, since it is not possible to find any "*single figure* of a man, faultless in all its parts "and of exact proportion; your way is to collect, "from *several*, those members or features, which "are most perfect in each, and so, by joining "them together, to compound one whole body, "completely beautiful."—"That is our method."—"What then, continued Socrates, and "are you not able, also, to imitate in colours, the

"MANNERS;

" MANNERS; those tendencies and dispositions of " the soul, which are benevolent, friendly, and " amiable; such as inspire love and affection " into the heart, and whose soft insinuations " carry with them the power of persuasion?"

" How, replied Parrhasius, can the pencil " imitate *that*, which hath no proportion, co-" lour, or any other of those properties, you " have been just now enumerating, as the objects " of sight?"—" Why, is it not true, returned " Socrates, that a man sometimes casts a *kind*, " sometimes an *angry*, look on others?"—" It is." —" There must then be something in the eyes " capable of expressing those passions."—" There " must."—" And is there not a wide difference " between the look of him, who takes part in " the prosperity of a friend, and another, who " sympathizes with him in his sorrows?"—" Un-" doubtedly, there is the widest. The counte-" nance, in the one case, expresses joy, in the " other, concern."—" These affections may then " be represented in picture."—" They may so." " In like manner, all other dispositions of our " nature, *the lofty and the liberal, the abject and* " *ungenerous, the temperate and the prudent, the* " *petulant and profligate*, these are severally dis-" cernible by the *look or attitude:* and that, whe-" ther we observe men in *action*, or at *rest*. " They " are."—" And these, therefore, come within

" the

"the power of graphical imitation?"—"They "do."—"Which then, concluded Socrates, do "you believe, men take the greatest pleasure in "contemplating; such imitations, as set before "them the GOOD, the LOVELY, and the FAIR, "or those, which represent the BAD, the "HATEFUL, and the UGLY, *qualities and affections of humanity?*"—"There can be no doubt, "said Parrhasius, of their giving the preference "to the former." [Lib. iii.]

The conclusion, the *philosopher* drives at in this conversation, and which the *painter* readily concedes to him, is what, I am perfeaded, every master of the art would be willing to act upon, were he at liberty to pursue the bent of his natural genius and inclination. But it unfortunately happens, to the infinite prejudice of this *mode of imitation*, above all others, that the artist *designs* not so much what the dignity of his profession requires of him, or the general taste of those he would most wish for his judges, approves; as what the rich or noble *connoisseur*, who *bespeaks* his work, and prescribes the subject, demands. What this has usually been, let the history of ancient and modern painting declare [q]. Yet, considering its vast power

[q] There having been such wretches, as the painter Plutarch speaks of—[illegible] De aud. Poët.

in

in MORALS, as explained above, one cannot enough lament the ill deſtiny of this divine ART; which, from the chaſte hand-maid of *virtue*, hath been debauched, in violence to her nature, to a ſhameleſs proſtitute of *vice*, and procureſs of *pleaſure*.

117. SCRIBIMUS INDOCTI DOCTIQUE POEMATA PASSIM.] The DOCTI POETAE have at all times been eſteemed by the wiſe and good, or, rather, have been reverenced, as Plato ſpeaks, ὥσπερ πατέρες τῆς σοφίας καὶ ἡγεμόνες.

As for the INDOCTI, we may take their character as drawn by the ſevere, but juſt, pen of our great Milton—— "Poëtas equidem verè "dictos et diligo et colo et audiendo ſaepiſſimè "delector—iſtos verò verſiculorum nugivendos "quis non oderit? quo genere nihil ſtultius "aut vanius aut corruptius, aut mendacius. "Laudant, vituperant, ſine delectu, ſine diſ-"crimine, judicio aut modo, nunc principes, "nunc plebeios, doctos juxta atque indoctos, "probos an improbos perindè habent; prout "cantharus, aut ſpes nummuli, aut fatuus ille "furor inflat ac rapit; congeſtis undique et "verborum et rerum tot diſcoloribus ineptiis "tamque putidis, ut laudatum longè praeſtet "ſileri, et pravo, quod aiunt, vivere naſo, "quàm ſic laudari: vituperatus verò qui ſit, "haud

"haud mediocri sanè honori sibi ducat, se tam "absurdis, tam stolidis nebulonibus displicere." DEF. SECUND. PRO POP. ANG. p. 337. 4to. Lond. 1753.

118. HIC ERROR TAMEN, &c.] What follows from hence to line 136, containing an encomium on *the office of poets*, is one of the leading beauties in the epistle. Its artifice consists in this, that, under the cover of a negligent commendation, interspersed with even some *traits* of pleasantry upon them, it insinuates to the emperor, in the manner the least offensive and ostentatious, the genuine merits, and even *sacredness* of their character. The whole is a fine instance of that address, which, in delivering rules for this kind of writing, the poet prescribes elsewhere:

Et sermone opus est modo tristi, saepe jocoso,
Defendente vicem modo rhetoris atque poëtae;
Interdum URBANI PARCENTIS VIRIBUS ATQUE
EXTENUANTIS EAS CONSULTO. [I S. x. 14.]

This conduct, in the place before us, shews the poet's exquisite knowledge of *human nature*. For there is no surer method of removing prejudices, and gaining over *others* to an esteem of any thing we would recommend, than by not appearing to lay too great a stress on it *ourselves*.

&c

It is, further, a proof of his intimate acquaintance with the peculiar turn of the *great*; who, not being forward to think highly of any thing but themſelves and their own dignities, are, with difficulty, brought to conceive of other accompliſhments, as of much value; and can only be won by the fair and candid addreſs of their apologiſt, who muſt be ſure not to carry his praiſes and pretenſions too high. It is this art of entering into the *characters, prejudices, and expectations* of others, and of knowing to ſuit our application, prudently, but with innocence, to them, which conſtitutes what we call A KNOWLEDGE OF THE WORD. An art, of which the great poet was a conſummate maſter, and than which there cannot be a more uſeful or amiable quality. Only we muſt take care not to confound it with that ſupple, verſatile, and intriguing genius, which, taking all ſhapes, and reflecting all characters, generally paſſes for it in the commerce of the world, or rather is prized much above it; but, as requiring no other talents in the poſſeſſor, than thoſe of a *low cunning* and *corrupt deſign*, is of all others the moſt miſchievous, worthleſs, and contemptible character, that infeſts human life.

118. HIC ERROR TAMEN ET LEVIS HAEC INSANIA QUANTAS VIRTUTES HABEAT, SIC COLLIGE:]

COLLEGE.] This apology for *poets*, and, in them, for *poetry* itself, though delivered with much apparent negligence and unconcern, yet, if considered, will be found to comprize in it every thing, that any, or all, of its most zealous advocates have ever pretended in its behalf. For it comprehends,

I. [From line 118 to 124,] THE PERSONAL GOOD QUALITIES OF THE POET. Nothing is more insisted on by those, who take upon themselves the patronage and recommendation of any *art*, than that it tends to raise in the professor of it all those *virtues*, which contribute most to his *own* proper enjoyment, and render him most agreeable to *others*. Now this, it seems, may be urged, on the side of *poetry*, with a peculiar force. For not only the *study* of this art hath a *direct* tendency to produce a neglect or disregard of *worldly honours and emoluments* (from the too eager appetite of which almost all the *calamities*, as well as the more unfriendly *vices*, of men arise) but he, whom the benign aspect of the muse hath glanced upon, and destined for her peculiar service, is, by *constitution*, which is ever the best security, fortified against the attacks of them. Thus his RAPTURES in the enjoyment of his muse make him overlook *the common accidents of life*: [line 121] *he is generous, open, and undesigning, by* NATURE: [line 122] to which we muſt not forget to add, that he is *temperate*, that is to ſay, *poor*, by PROFESSION.

VIVIT SILIQUIS ET PANE SECUNDO.

II. [From line 124 to 132.] THE UTILITY OF THE POET TO THE STATE: and this both on a *civil* and *moral* account. For, 1. the poets, whom we read in our younger years, and from whom we learn the *power of words*, and *hidden harmony of numbers*, that is, as a profound Scotchman teaches, the *firſt and moſt eſſential principles* of eloquence [*r*], enable, by degrees, and inſtruct their pupil to appear, with advantage, in that extenſively uſeful capacity of a public ſpeaker. And, indeed, graver writers than our poet have ſent the orator to this ſchool. But the pretenſions of poetry go much farther. It delights [from line 130 to 132] to immortalize the triumphs of virtue: to *record* or *feign* illuſtrious examples of heroic worth, for the ſervice of the *riſing age*: and, which is the laſt and beſt fruit of philoſophy itſelf, it can relieve even the languor of *ill-health*, and ſuſtain *poverty* herſelf under the ſcorn and inſult of contumelious opulence. 2. In a *moral* view its ſervices are not leſs conſiderable. (For it may be obſerved the *poet* was ſo far of a mind with the *philoſopher*,

[*r*] See an Eſſay on the *Compoſition of the Antients*, by J. GEDDES, Eſq;

to

to give no quarter to *immoral* poets). And to this end it serves, 1. [line 127] *in turning the ear of youth* from that early corruptor of its innocence, the seducement of a *loose and impure communication*. 2. Next [line 128] in forming our riper age (which it does with all the address and tenderness of *friendship*: AMICIS *praeceptis*) *by the sanctity and wisdom of its precepts*. And, 3. which is the proper office of *tragedy*, in *correcting the excesses of the natural passions* [line 122]. The reader who doth not turn himself to the original, will be apt to mistake this detail of the virtues of poetry, for an account of the policy and legislation of ancient and modern times; whose proudest boast, when the philanthropy of their enthusiastic projectors ran at the highest, was but to *prevent the impressions of vice*: to *form the mind to habits of virtue*: and *to curb and regulate the passions*.

III. HIS SERVICES TO RELIGION. This might well enough be said, whether by *religion* we understand an *internal reverence* of the gods, which poetry first and principally intended; or their *popular education and worship*, which, by its *fictions*, as of necessity conforming to the received fancies of superstition, it must greatly tend to promote and establish. But the poet, artfully seizing a circumstance, which supposes and includes in it both these respects, renders his defence vastly interesting.

All the customary *addresses* of heathenism to its gods, more especially on any great and solemn emergency, were the work of the poet. For *nature*, it seems, had taught the pagan world, what the Hebrew prophets themselves did not disdain to practise, that, to lift the imagination, and, with it, the sluggish affections of human nature, to heaven, it was expedient to lay hold on every assistance of art. They therefore presented their supplications to the divinity in the richest and brightest dress of eloquence, which is poetry. Not to insist, that *devotion*, when sincere and ardent, from its very *nature*, enkindles a glow of thought, which communicates strongly with the transports of poetry. Hence *the language of the gods* (for so was poetry accounted, as well from its being the divinest species of communication, our rude conceptions can well frame even for superior intelligencies, as for that it was the fittest vehicle of our applications to them) became not the ornament only, but an *essential* in the ceremonial, of paganism. And this, together with an allusion to *a form of public prayer* (for such was his *secular ode)* composed by himself, gives, at once, a grace and sublimity to this part of the apology, which are perfectly inimitable.

Thus

Thus hath the great poet, in the compass of a few lines, drawn together a complete defence of his *art*. For what more could the warmest admirer of poetry, or, because zeal is quickened by opposition, what more could the vehement declaimer against Plato (who proscribed it), urge in its behalf, than that it furnishes, to the poet himself, the surest means of *solitary and social* enjoyment: and farther serves to the most important CIVIL, MORAL, and RELIGIOUS purposes?

119. — VATIS AVARUS NON TEMERE EST ANIMUS.] There is an unlucky Italian proverb, which says, *Chi ben scrive, non sara mai ricco.*—The true reason, without doubt, is here given by the poet.

124. MILITIAE QUAMQUAM PIGER ET MALUS.] The observation has much grace, as referring to himself, who had acquired no credit, as a soldier, in the civil wars of his country.—We have an example of this misalliance between the *poetic* and *military* character, recorded in the history of our own civil wars, which may be just worth mentioning. Sir P. Warwick, speaking of the famous Earl of *Newcastle*, observes—"his edge had too much "of the razor in it; for he had a tincture of a

"romantic ſpirit, and had the misfortune to "have ſomewhat of the poet in him; ſo as he "choſe Sir William Davenant, an eminent "good poet, and loyal gentleman, to be lieu-"tenant-general of his ordnance. This inclina-"tion of his own, and ſuch kind of witty ſo-"ciety (to be modeſt in the expreſſions of it) "diverted many councils, and loſt many oppor-"tunities, which the nature of that affair, this "great man had now entered into, required." MEMOIRS, p. 235.

132. CASTIS CUM PUERIS, &c.] We have, before, taken notice, how properly the poet, for the eaſier and more ſucceſsful introduction of his apology, aſſumed the perſon *urbani, parcentis viribus*. We ſee him here, in *that* of *rhetoris atque poetae*. For admoniſhed, as it were, by the riſing dignity of his ſubject, which led him from the *moral*, to ſpeak of the *religious* uſes of poetry, he inſenſibly drops the *badineur*, and takes an air, not of ſeriouſneſs only, but of ſolemnity. This change is made with *art*. For the attention is carried from the uſes of poetry, in *conſoling the unhappy*, by the eaſieſt tranſition imaginable, to the ſtill more ſolemn application of it to the *offices of piety*. And its *uſe* is, to impreſs on the mind a ſtronger ſenſe of the weight of the poet's plea, than could have been expected

expected from a more direct and continued declamation. For this is the constant and natural effect of knowing to pass from *gay* to *severe*, with grace and dignity.

169. SED HABET COMOEDIA TANTO PLUS ONERIS, QUANTO VENIAE MINUS.] Tragedy, whose intention is to *affect*, may secure what is most essential to its *kind*, though it fail in some minuter resemblances of *nature*: Comedy, proposing for its main end *exact representation*, is fundamentally defective, if it do not perfectly succeed in it. And this explains the ground of the poet's observation, that comedy hath *veniae minus*; for he is speaking of the draught of the *manners* only, in which respect a greater *indulgence* is very deservedly shewn to the tragic than comic writer. But though tragedy hath thus far the advantage, yet, in another respect, its laws are more severe than those of comedy; and that is in the conduct of the *fable*. It may be asked then, which of the two dramas is, on the whole, most difficult. To which the answer is decisive. For tragedy, whose end is the *pathos*, produces it by *action*, while comedy produces its end, the *humourous*, by *character*. Now it is much more difficult to paint manners, than to plan action; because *that* requires the

philoſopher's knowledge of human nature; *this*, only the hiſtorian's knowledge of human events.

It is true, in one ſenſe, the *tragic* muſe has *veniae minus*; for though grave and pleaſant ſcenes may be indifferently repreſented, or even mixed together, in comedy, yet, in tragedy, the ſerious and ſolemn air muſt prevail throughout. Indeed, our Shakeſpeare has violated this rule, as he hath, upon occaſion, almoſt every other rule, of juſt criticiſm: Whence, ſome writers, taking advantage of that idolatrous admiration which is generally profeſſed for this great poet, and nauſeating, I ſuppoſe, the more common, though juſter, forms of literary compoſition, have been for turning his very tranſgreſſion of the principles of common ſenſe, into a ſtanding precept for the ſtage. "It is ſaid, that, if "comedy may be wholly *ſerious*, why may not "tragedy now and then be indulged in being "*gay?*" If theſe critics be in earneſt, in putting this queſtion, they need not long wait for an anſwer. The *end* of comedy being *to paint the manners*, nothing hinders (as I have ſhewn at large in the diſſertation *on the provinces of the drama)* but "that it may take either character "of *pleaſant* or *ſerious*, as it chances, or even "unite them both in one piece:" But the end of tragedy being *to excite the ſtronger paſſions*, this diſcordancy in the ſubject breaks the flow

of

of those passions, and so prevents, or lessens at least, the very effect which this drama primarily intends. "It is said, indeed, that this contrast "of *grave* and *pleasant* scenes, heightens the "*passion*:" if it had been said that it heightens the *surprize*, the observation had been more just. Lastly, "we are told, that this is nature, "which generally blends together the *ludicrous* "and the *sublime*." But who does not know

That art is nature to advantage dress'd;

and that to dress our nature *to advantage* in the present instance, that is, in a composition whose laws are to be deduced from the consideration of its *end*, these characters are to be kept, by an artist, perfectly distinct?

However, this restraint upon tragedy does not prove that, upon the whole, it has *plus oneris*. All I can allow is, that either drama has *weight* enough, in all reason, for the ablest *shoulders* to sustain.

177. QUEM TULIT AD SCENAM VENTOSO GLORIA CURRU, EXANIMAT LENTUS SPECTATOR, &c. to line 182.] There is an exquisite spirit of pleasantry in these lines, which hath quite evaporated in the hands of the critics. These have gravely supposed them to come from the *person* of the *poet*, and to contain his serious censure of the vanity of poetic fame. Whereas, besides

besides the manifest absurdity of the thing, its inconsistency with what is delivered elsewhere on this subject [A. P. line 324.] where the Greeks are commended as being *praeter laudem nullius avari*, absolutely requires us to understand them as proceeding from an *objector*; who, as the poet hath very satirically contrived, is left to expose himself in the very terms of his *objection*. He had just been blaming the venality of the Roman dramatic writers. They had shewn themselves more sollicitous about *filling their pockets*, than deserving the reputation of good poets. And, instead of insisting further on the excellency of this *latter* motive, he stops short, and brings in a bad poet himself to laugh at it.

" And, what then, says he, you would have " us yield ourselves to the very wind and gust " of praise; and, dropping all inferior con- " siderations, drive away to the expecting stage " in the *puffed car of vain-glory?* For what? " To be *dispirited*, or blown up with air, as the " capricious spectator shall think fit to enforce " or withhold his *inspirations*. And is this the " mighty benefit of your vaunted passion for " fame? No; farewel the stage, if the breath " of others is *that*, on which the silly bard is " to depend for the contraction or enlargement " of his dimensions." To all which convincing rhetoric, the poet condescends to say nothing;

as

as well knowing, that no truer service is, oftentimes, done to virtue or good sense, than when a knave or fool is left to himself, to employ his idle raillery against either.

These interlocutory passages, laying open the sentiments of those against whom the poet is disputing, are very frequent in the *critical and moral* writings of Horace, and are well suited to their dramatic genius and original.

210. ILLE PER EXTENTUM FUNEM, &c.] The Romans, who were immoderately addicted to spectacles of every kind, had in particular esteem the *funambuli*, or *rope-dancers*:

> *Ita populus studio stupidus in* FUNAMBULO
> *Animum occuparat.* PROL. in HECYR.

From the admiration of whose tricks the expression, *ire per extentum funem*, came to denote, proverbially, *an uncommon degree of excellence and perfection in any thing*. The allusion is, here, made with much pleasantry, as the poet had just been railing their fondness for these *extraordinary atchievements*.

Ibid. ILLE PER EXTENTUM FUNEM, &c. to line 214.] It is observable, that Horace, here, makes his own *feeling* the test of poetical merit. Which is said with a philosophical exactness.

For the *pathos* in tragic, *humour* in comic, and the ſame holds of the *ſublime* in the narrative, and of every other *ſpecies* of excellence in univerſal poetry, is the object not of *reaſon*, but *ſentiment*; and can be eſtimated only from its *impreſſion* on the mind, not by any ſpeculative or general *rules*. Rules themſelves are indeed nothing elſe but an appeal to *experience*; concluſions drawn from wide and general obſervation of the aptneſs and efficacy of certain *means* to produce thoſe *impreſſions*. So that feeling or ſentiment itſelf is not only the ſureſt but the ſole *ultimate* arbiter of works of genius.

Yet, though this be true, the *invention* of *general rules* is not without its merit, nor the *application* of them without its *uſe*, as may appear from the following conſiderations.

It may be affirmed, univerſally, of all *didactic writing*, that it is employed in *referring particular facts to general principles*. General principles themſelves can often be referred to others more general; and theſe again carried ſtill higher, till we come to a *ſingle* principle, in which all the reſt are involved. When this is done, ſcience of every kind hath attained its higheſt perfection.

The account, here given, might be illuſtrated from various inſtances. But it will be ſufficient to confine ourſelves to the ſingle one of

criticiſm;

criticiſm; by which I underſtand that *ſpecies* of didactic writing, which *refers to general rules the virtues and faults of compoſition*. And the perfection of this *art* would conſiſt in an ability to refer *every* beauty and blemiſh to a ſeparate claſs; and *every* claſs, by a gradual progreſſion, to ſome *one* ſingle principle. But the *art* is, as yet, far ſhort of perfection. For many of theſe beauties and blemiſhes can be referred to no general rule at all; and the rules, which have been diſcovered, ſeem many of them unconnected, and not reducible to a common principle. It muſt be admitted, however, that ſuch critics are employed in their proper office, as contribute to the *confirmation* of rules already eſtabliſhed, or the *invention* of new ones.

Rules already eſtabliſhed are then *confirmed*, when more *particulars* are referred to them. The invention of *new* rules implies, 1. A *collection* of various particulars, not yet regulated. 2. A *diſcovery* of thoſe circumſtances of *reſemblance* or *agreement*, whereby they become capable of being regulated. And, 3. A ſubſequent *regulation* of them, or arrangement into *one* claſs according to *ſuch* circumſtances of *agreement*. When this is done, the rule is completed. But if the critic is not able to obſerve any *common* circumſtance of reſemblance in the ſeveral particulars he hath collected, by which they may, all of them,

them, be referred to one general clafs, he hath then made no advancement in the *art of criticifm*. Yet the collection of his particular obfervations may be of ufe to other critics; juft as collections of natural hiftory, though no part of philofophy, may yet affift philofophical enquirers.

We fee then from this general view of the matter, that the *merit* of inventing *general rules* confifts in reducing criticifm to an *art*; and that the *ufe* of applying them, in practice, when the art is thus formed, is, to direct the caprices of *tafte* by the authority of rule, which we call *reafon*.

And, thus much being premifed, we fhall now be able to form a proper judgment of the *method*, which fome of the moft admired of the antients, as well as moderns, have taken in this *work of criticizing*. The moft eminent, at leaft the moft popular, are, perhaps, Longinus, of the Greeks; P. Bouhours, of the French; and Mr. Addifon, with us in England.

1. *All* the beautiful paffages, which LONGINUS cites, are referred by him to *five* general claffes. And, 2dly, Thefe general claffes belong all to the *common* principle of *fublimity*. He does not fay this paffage is *excellent*, but affigns the *kind* of excellence, *viz. fublimity*. Neither does he content himfelf with the general notion of *fublimity*, but names the *fpecies*, viz. *Grandeur* of *fentiment*,

ment, power of moving the *passions*, &c. His work therefore enables us to *class* our perceptions of excellence, and consequently is formed on the *true plan* of criticism.

2. The same may be observed of P. BOUHOURS. The passages, cited by him, are never mentioned *in general* terms as *good* or *bad*: but are instances of good or bad *sentiment*. This is the *genus*, in which *all* his instances are comprehended: but of this genus he marks also the distinct *species*. He does not say, this sentiment is *good*; but it is *sublime*, or *natural*, or *beautiful*, or *delicate*: or, that another sentiment is *bad*; but that it is *mean*, or *false*, or *deformed*, or *affected*. To these several classes he refers his particular instances: and these classes themselves are referred to the more comprehensive principles of the excellence or fault of *single sentiment*, as opposed to the various *other* excellences and faults, which are observed in composition.

3. Mr. ADDISON, in his *criticism on Milton*, proceeded in like manner. For, *first*, these remarks are evidently applicable to the general observations on the poem; in which every thing is referred to the common heads of *fable*, *morals*, *sentiments*, and *language*; and even the *specific* excellences and faults considered under each head distinctly marked out. *Secondly*, The same is true concerning *many* of the observations on particular

particular passages. The reader is not only told, that a passage *has* merit; but is informed what *sort* of merit belongs to it.

Neither are the remaining observations wholly without use. For such particular beauties and blemishes, as are barely *collected*, may yet serve as a foundation to future enquirers for making further discoveries. They may be considered as so many *single* facts, an *attention* to which is excited by the authority of the critic; and when these are considered jointly with such as *others* may have observed, those general principles of *similitude* may at length be found, which shall enable us to constitute *new* classes of poetical merit or blame.

Thus far the candid reader may go in apologizing for the *merits* of these writers. But as, in sound criticism, candour must not be indulged at the expence of *justice*, I think myself obliged to add an observation concerning their *defects*; and *that*, on what I must think the just principles here delivered.

Though the method, taken by these writers, be *scientifical*, the real service they have done to criticism is not very considerable. And the reason is, they dwell too much in *generals*: that is, not only the *genus*, to which they refer their *species*, is too large, but those very subordinate species themselves are too comprehensive.

Of

Of the *three* critics, under consideration, the most instructive is, unquestionably, *Longinus.* The *genus* itself, under which he ranks his several *classes*, is as *particular*, as the species of the other two. Yet even *his* classes are much too general to convey any very distinct and useful information. It had been still better, if this fine critic had descended to lower and more minute *particularities*, as subordinate to *each class*. For to observe of any *sentiment*, that it is *grand*, or *pathetic*, and so of the other *species* of sublime, is saying very little. Few readers want to be informed of this. It had been sufficient, if any notice was to be taken at all of so *general* beauties, to have done it in the way, which some of the best critics have taken, of merely pointing to them. But could he have discovered, and produced to observation, those *peculiar* qualities in *sentiment*, which occasion the impression of *grandeur*, *pathos*, &c. this had been advancing the science of criticism very much, as tending to lay open the more secret and hidden springs of that *pleasure*, which results from poetical composition.

P. Bouhours, as I observed, is still more faulty: His very *species* are so large, as make his criticism almost wholly useless and insignificant.

It gives one pain to refuse to such a writer, as Mr. *Addison*, any *kind* of merit, which he appears to have valued himſelf upon, and which the generality of his readers have ſeemed willing to allow him. Yet it muſt not be diſſembled, that *criticiſm* was by no means his talent. His taſte was truly elegant; but he had neither that vigour of underſtanding, nor chaſtiſed, philoſophical ſpirit, which are ſo eſſential to this character, and which we find in hardly any of the antients beſides Ariſtotle, and but in a very few of the moderns. For what concerns his *criticiſm on Milton* in particular, there was this accidental benefit ariſing from it, that it occaſioned an admirable poet to be read, and his excellencies to be obſerved. But for the merit of the work itſelf, if there be any thing juſt in the *plan*, it was, becauſe Ariſtotle and Boſſu had taken the ſame route before him. And as to his *own* proper obſervations, they are for the moſt part ſo general and indeterminate, as to afford but little inſtruction to the reader, and are, not unfrequently, altogether frivolous. They are of a kind with thoſe, in which the French critics (for I had rather inſtance in the defects of *foreign* writers than of our *own*) ſo much abound; and which good judges agree to rank in the worſt ſort of criticiſm. To give one example for all.

Cardinal Perron, taking occaſion to commend certain pieces of the poet Ronsard, chuſes

chuses to deliver himself in the following manners: "Prenez de lui quelque poëme que ce "soit, il paye toujours son lecteur, et quand la "verve le prend, il se guinde en haut, il vous "porte jusques dans les nuës, il vous fait voir "mille belles choses.

"Que ses *saisons* sont *bien-faites!* Que la "description de la lyre a Bertaut est *admirable!* "Que le discours au ministre, *excellent!* Tous "ses hymnes sont *beaux*. Celui de l'eternité "est *admirable*; ceux des saisons *marveilleux*." [Perroniana.]

What now has the reader learned from this varied criticism, but that his *Eminence* was indeed very fond of his poet; and that he esteemed these several pieces to be (what with less expence of words he might, in one breath, have called them) *well-turned*, *beautiful*, *excellent*, *admirable*, *marvellous*, poems? To have given us the true character of *each*, and to have marked the precise *degree*, as well as *kind*, of merit in these works, had been a task of another nature.

211. — QUI PECTUS INANITER ANGIT.] The word *inaniter*, as well as *falsi*, applied in the following line to *terrores*, would express that wondrous force of *dramatic representation*, which compels us to take part in *feigned* adventures and situations, as if they were *real*; and exer-

ciſes the paſſions with the ſame violence, in *remote fancied ſcenes*, as in the *preſent diſtreſſes of real life*.

And this is that ſovereign quality in poetry, which, as an old writer of our own naturally expreſſes it, is of force *to hold children from play, and old men from the chimney corner* [*s*]. The poet, in the place before us, conſiders it as a kind of *magic virtue*, which tranſports the ſpectator into all *places*, and makes him, occaſionally, aſſume all *perſons*. The reſemblance holds, alſo, in this, that its effects are inſtantaneous and irreſiſtible. *Rules*, *art*, *decorum*, all fall before it. It goes directly to the *heart*, and gains all purpoſes at once. Hence it is, that, ſpeaking of a real genius, poſſeſſed of this commanding power, Horace pronounces him, emphatically, THE POET,

> *Ille per extentum funem mihi poſſe videtur*
> *Ire* POETA:

it being more eſpecially this property, which, of itſelf, diſcovers the *true dramatiſt*, and ſecures the ſucceſs of his performance, not only without the aſſiſtance of *art*, but in direct oppoſition to its clearest dictates.

This power has been felt on a thouſand other occaſions. But its triumphs were never more

[*s*] Sir Philip Sidney.

conſpicuous,

conſpicuous, than in the famous inſtance of the CID of P. Corneille; which, by the ſole means of this enchanting quality, drew along with it the affections and applauſes of a whole people; notwithſtanding the manifeſt tranſgreſſion of ſome eſſential rules, the utmoſt tyranny of jealous power, and, what is more, in defiance of all the authority and good ſenſe of one of the juſteſt pieces of criticiſm in the French language, written purpoſely to diſcredit and expoſe it.

224. CUM LAMENTAMUR NON ADPARERE LABORES NOSTROS, &c.] It was remarked upon line 211, that the beauties of a poem can only *appear* by being felt. And *they*, to whom they do not appear in this inſtance, are the writer's own *friends*, who, it is not to be ſuppoſed, would diſguiſe their *feelings*. So that the *lamentation*, here ſpoken of, is at once a proof of *impertinence* in the poet, and of the *badneſs* of his poetry, which ſets the complainant in a very ridiculous light.

228. EGERE VETES.] The poet intended, in theſe words, a very juſt ſatire on thoſe preſuming *wits and ſcholars*, who, under the pretence of getting above diſtreſsful *want*, in reality aſpire to public honours and preferments; though

this be the most inexcusable of all follies (to give it the softest name), which can infest a man of letters: Both, because experience, on which a wise man would chuse to regulate himself, is contrary to these hopes; and because, if literary merit could succeed in them, the *reward*, as the poet speaks,

would either bring
No joy, or be destructive of the thing:

That is, the learned would either have no relish for the delights of so widely different a situation; or, which hath oftener been the case, would lose the learning itself, or the *love* of it at least, on which their pretensions to this *reward* are founded.

232. GRATUS ALEXANDRO REGI MAGNO, &c.] This praise of Augustus, arising from the comparison of his character with that of Alexander, is extremely fine. It had been observed of the Macedonian by his historians and panegyrists, that, to the stern virtues of the *conqueror*, he had joined the softer accomplishments of the *virtuoso*, in a just discernment and love of *poetry*, and of the *elegant arts*. The one was thought clear, from his admiration and study of Homer: And the *other*, from his famous edict concerning Apelles and Lysippus, could not be denied. Horace finds means to turn both these

circumstances

circumſtances in his ſtory to the advantage of his prince.

From his extravagant pay of ſuch a wretched verſifier as *Chœrilus*, he would inſinuate, that Alexander's love of the muſe was, in fact, but a blind unintelligent impulſe towards *glory*. And from his greater ſkill in the arts of *ſculpture* and *painting*, than of *verſe*, he repreſents him as more concerned about the *drawing* of his figure, than the pourtraiture of his *manners and mind*. Whereas Auguſtus, by his liberalities to *Varius* and *Virgil*, had diſcovered the trueſt taſte in the *art*, from which he expected immortality: and, in truſting to *that*, as the *chief* inſtrument of his fame, had confeſſed a prior regard to thoſe *mental virtues*, which are the real ornament of humanity, before that *look of terror*, and *air and attitude of victory*, in which the brute violence of Alexander moſt delighted to be ſhewn.

243. MUSARUM DONA.] The expreſſion is happy; as implying, that theſe *images* of virtue, which are repreſented as of ſuch importance to the glory of princes, are not the mere *offerings* of poetry to greatneſs, but the *free-gifts* of the muſe to the poet. For it is only to ſuch *works*, as theſe, that Horace attributes the wondrous efficacy of expreſſing the *manners and mind* in

 fuller

fuller and more durable relief, than *sculpture* gives to the *exterior figure*.

> *Non magis expressi vultus per aënea signa,*
> *Quam per vatis opus mores animique virorum*
> *Clarorum adparent.*

247.—VIRGILIUS.] Virgil is mentioned, in this place, simply as a *poet*. The precise idea of his *poetry* is given us elsewhere.

> *molle atque facetum*
> *Virgilio annuerunt gaudentes rure Camaenae.*
> [1 Sat. x. 44.

But this may appear a strange praise of the sweet and polished Virgil. It may appear so to Quinctilian, who cites this passage, and explains it, without doubt, very justly, yet in such a way as shews that he was not quite certain of the truth of his explanation.

The case, I believe, was this. The word *facetum*, which makes the difficulty, had acquired, in Quinctilian's days, the sense of *pleasant, witty*, or *facetious, in exclusion* to every other idea, which had formerly belonged to it. It is true that, in the Augustan age, and still earlier, *facetum* was sometimes used in this sense. But its proper and original meaning was no more than *exact, factitatum, benè factum*. And in this strict sense, I believe, it is always used by Horace.

Malthinus

Malthinus tunicis demissis ambulat: est qui
Inguen ad obscoenum subductis usque facetus.

1 Sat. II. 25.

i. e. *tucked up, trim, expedite.*

Mutatis tantùm pedibus numerisque facetus.

1 Sat. IV. 7.

i. e. he [Lucilius] adopted a *stricter* measure, than the writers of the old comedy; or, by changing the loose iambic to the hexameter verse, he gave a proof his *art, skill,* and *improved judgment.*

frater, pater, adde;
Ut cuique est aetas, ita quemque facetus *adopta.*

1 Ep. VI. 55.

i. e. *nicely* and *accurately* adapt your address to the age and condition of each.

I do not recollect any other place where *facetus* is used by Horace; and in all these it seems probable to me that the principal idea, conveyed by it, is that of *care, art, skill,* only differently modified according to the subject to which it is applied: a gown tucked up *with care*—a measure *studiously* affected—an address *nicely* accommodated—No thought of *ridicule* or *pleasantry* intended.

It is the same in the present instance—

MOLLE ATQUE FACETUM,

i. e.

i. e. *a soft flowing versification*, and *an exquisitely finished expression:* the two precise, characteristic merits of Virgil's *rural* poetry.

This change, in the sense of words, is common in all languages, and creeps in so gradually and imperceptibly as to elude the notice, sometimes, of the best critics, even in their own language. The transition of ideas, in the present instance, may be traced thus. As what was *wittily* said, was most *studied*, *artificial*, and *exquisite*; hence in process of time *facetum* lost its primary sense, and came to signify merely, *witty*.

We have a like example in our own language. A *good wit* meant formerly a man of good natural sense and understanding: but because what we now call *wit* was observed to be the flower and quintessence, as it were, of good sense, hence *a man of wit* is now the exclusive attribute of one who exerts his good sense in that peculiar manner.

247. DILECTI TIBI VIRGILIUS, &c.] It does honour to the memory of Augustus, that he bore the *affection*, here spoken of, to this amiable poet; who was not more distinguished from his contemporary writers by the force of an original, inventive genius, than the singular benevolence and humanity of his character. Yet there

there have been critics of so perverse a turn, as to discover an inclination, at least, of disputing both.

1. Some have taken offence at his supposed unfriendly neglect of Horace, who, on every occasion, shewed himself so ready to lavish all his praises on him. But the folly of this slander is of a piece with its malignity, as proceeding on the absurd fancy, that Virgil's friends might as easily have slid into such works, as the Georgics and Eneis, as those of Horace into the various occasional poems, which employed his pen.

Just such another senseless suspicion hath been raised of his jealousy of Homer's superior glory (a vice, from which the nature of the great poet was singularly abhorrent), only because he did not think fit to give him the first place among the poets in *Elysium*, several hundred years before he had so much as made his appearance upon *earth*.

But these petty calumnies of his *moral* character hardly deserve a confutation. What some greater authorities have objected to his *poetical*, may be thought more serious. For,

2. It has been given out by some of better note among the moderns, and from thence, according to the customary influence of authority, hath become the prevailing sentiment of the

generality

generality of the learned, that the great poet was more indebted for his fame to the *exactness of his judgment; to his industry, and a certain trick of imitation*, than to the energy of natural genius; which he is thought to have possessed in a very slender degree.

This charge is founded on the similitude, which all acknowledge, betwixt his great work, the Aeneïs, and the poems of Homer. But, "how far such similitude infers imitation; or, "how far imitation itself infers an inferiority "of natural genius in the imitator," this hath never been considered. In short, the affair of *imitation* in poetry, though one of the most curious and interesting in all criticism, hath been, hitherto, very little understood: as may appear from hence, that there is not, as far as I can learn, one single treatise, now extant, written purposely to explain it; the discourse, which the learned *Menage* intended, and which, doubtless, would have given light to this matter, having never, as I know of, been made public. To supply, in some measure, this loss, I have thought it not amiss to put together, and methodize a few reflexions of my own on this subject, which (because the matter is large, and cannot easily be drawn into a compass that suits with the nature of these occasional remarks) the reader will find in a distinct and seperate dissertation upon it [t].

CONCLUSION.

And, now, having explained, in the best manner I could, the two famous Epistles of Horace to Augustus and the Pisos, it may be expected, in conclusion, that I should say something of the rest of our poet's critical writings. For his *Sermones* (under which general term I include his *Epistles*) are of two sorts, MORAL and CRITICAL; and, though both are exquisite, the *latter* are, perhaps, in their kind, the more perfect of the two; his *moral* principles being sometimes, I believe, liable to exception; his *critical*, never.

The two pieces, illustrated in these volumes, are *strictly* critical: the *first*, being a professed criticism of the Roman drama; and the *last*, in order to their vindication, of the Roman poets. The rest of his works, which turn upon this subject of criticism, may be rather termed *Apologetical*. They are the IVth and Xth of the FIRST, and Ist of the SECOND book of Satires;

[t] Diss. III. in the third Volume.

and

and the XIXth of the FIRST, and, in part, the II[d] of the SECOND book of Epistles.

In *these*, the poet has THREE great objects; one or other of which he never loses sight of, and generally he prosecutes them all together, in the same piece. These objects are, 1. to vindicate the way of writing in satire. 2. To justify his opinion of a favourite writer of this class, the celebrated Lucilius. And, 3. to expose the careless and incorrect composition of the Roman writers.

He was himself deeply concerned in these three articles; so that he makes his own apology at the same time that he criticizes or censures others. The *address* of the poet's manner will be seen by bearing in mind this general purpose of his critical poetry. How he came to be *engaged* in this controversy, will best appear from a few observations on the state of the Roman learning, when he undertook to contribute his pains to the improvement of it.

I have, in the introduction to the first of these volumes, given a slight sketch of the rise and progress of the Roman satire. This poem was purely of Roman invention: *first of all* struck out of the old fescennine farce, and rudely cultivated, by Ennius: *Next*, more happily treated, and enriched with the best part of the

the old comedy, by Lucilius: And, after some succeeding essays, taken up and finally adorned, by Horace.

Horace was well known to the public by his lyric compositions, and still more perhaps by his favour at court, when he took upon him to correct the manners and taste of his age, by his *Lucilian Satires*. But, here, he encountered, at once, many prejudices; and all his own credit, together with that of his court-friends, was little enough to support him, against the torrent.

First, the kind of writing itself was sure to give offence. For, though men were well enough pleased to have their natural malignity gratified by an old poet's satire against a *former* age, yet they were naturally alarmed at the exercise of this talent upon their *own*, and, as it might chance, upon themselves.

The poet's eminence, and favour, would, besides, give a peculiar force and *effect* to his censures; so that all who found, or thought themselves liable to them, were concerned, in interest, to discredit the attempt, and blast his rising reputation.

Omnes hi metuunt versus, odere POETAM.

Hence, he was constrained to stand upon his own defence, and to vindicate, as well the thing itſelf, as his management of it, to the tender and ſuſpicious public.

But this was not all: For, SECONDLY, an old ſatiriſt, of high birth and quality, LUCILIUS, was conſidered, not only as an able writer of this claſs, but as a perfect model in it; and of courſe, therefore, this new ſatiriſt would be much decried and undervalued, on the compariſon. This circumſtance obliged the poet to reduce this admired writer to his real value; which could not be done without thwarting the general admiration, and pointing out his vices and defects in the freeſt manner. This perilous taſk he diſcharged in the IVth ſatire of his firſt book, and with ſuch rigour of criticiſm, that not only the partizans of Lucilius in the poet's own age, but the moſt knowing and candid critics of ſucceeding times, were diſpoſed to complain of it. However, the obnoxious ſtep had been taken; and nothing remained but to juſtify himſelf, as he hath done at large, in his Xth ſatire.

On the whole, in comparing what he has ſaid in theſe two ſatires with what Quinctilian long after obſerved on the ſubject of them, there ſeems no reaſon to conclude, that the poet judged ill: though he expreſſed his judgment in ſuch terms as he would, no doubt, have ſome-

thing

thing softened (out of complaisance to the general sentiment, and a becoming deference to the real merits of his master), if his adversaries had been more moderate in urging their charge, or if the occasion had not been so pressing.

Lastly, this attack on Lucilius produced, or rather involved in it, a THIRD quarrel. The poet's main objection to Lucilius was his careless, verbose, and hasty composition, which his admirers, no doubt, called genius, grace, and strength. This being an inveterate folly among his countrymen, he gives it no quarter. Through all his critical works, he employs the utmost force of his wit and good sense to expose it: And his own writings, being at the same time supremely correct, afforded his enemies (which would provoke them still more) no advantage against him. Yet they attempted, as they could, to repay his perpetual reproaches on the popular writers for their neglect of *limae labor*, by objecting to him, in their turn, that what he wrote was *sine nervis*: and this, though they felt his *force* themselves, and though another set of men were complaining, at the same time, of his *severity*,

> *Sunt quibus in satyrâ videor nimis* ACER—
> SINE NERVIS *altera quicquid*
> *Composui pars esse putat, similesque meorum*
> Mille die versus *deduci posse*—

His detractors satirically alluding, in these last words, to his charge against Lucilius —

in horâ *saepè* ducentos,
Ut magnum, versus *dictabat*, *stans pede in uno*.

It is not my purpose, in this place, to enlarge further on the character of Lucilius, whose *wordy* satires gave occasion to our poet's criticism. Several of the antient writers speak of him occasionally, in terms of the highest applause; and without doubt, he was a poet of distinguished merit. Yet it will hardly be thought, at this day, that it could be any discredit to him to be censured, rivalled, and excelled by Horace.

What I have here put together is only to furnish the young reader with the proper KEY to Horace's critical works, which generally turn on his own vindication, *against the enemies of satire — the admirers of Lucilius — and the patrons of loose and incorrect composition.*

In managing these several topics, he has found means to introduce a great deal of exquisite criticism. And though his scattered observations go but a little way towards making up a complete critical system, yet they are so *luminous*, as the French speak, that is, they are so replete with good sense, and extend so much farther than to the case to which they are immediately

mediately applied, that they furnish many of the principles on which such a system, if ever it be taken in hand, must be constructed: And, without carrying matters too far, we may safely affirm of these *Critical Discourses*, that, next to Aristotle's immortal work, they are the most valuable remains of antient art upon this subject.

The End of the Notes on the Epistle to AUGUSTUS.

CRITICAL DISSERTATIONS.

I. On the idea of universal poetry.

II. On the provinces of dramatic poetry.

III. On poetical imitation.

IV. On the marks of imitation.

VATIBVS ADDERE CALCAR,
VT STVDIO MAIORE PETANT HELICONA VIRENTEM.
Hor.

CRITICAL DISSERTATIONS.

I. On the idea of universal poetry.

II. On the provinces of dramatic poetry.

III. On poetical imitation.

IV. On the marks of imitation.

[illegible] arte,

[illegible] excludit sanos Helicone poetas.

Hor.

DISSERTATION I.

ON

THE IDEA OF UNIVERSAL POETRY.

WHEN we ſpeak of poetry, as an *art*, we mean *ſuch a way or method of treating a ſubject, as is found moſt pleaſing and delightful to us.* In all other kinds of literary compoſition, pleaſure is ſubordinate to USE: in poetry only, PLEASURE is the end, to which uſe itſelf (however it be, for certain reaſons, always pretended) muſt ſubmit.

This *idea* of the end of poetry is no novel one, but indeed the very ſame which our great philoſopher entertained of it; who gives it as the eſſential note of this part of learning—THAT IT SUBMITS THE SHEWS OF THINGS TO THE DESIRES OF THE MIND: WHEREAS REASON DOTH BUCKLE AND BOW THE MIND UNTO THE NATURE

NATURE OF THINGS. For to *gratify the deſires of the mind*, is to PLEASE: *Pleaſure* then, in the idea of Lord Bacon, is the ultimate and appropriate end of poetry; for the ſake of which it accommodates itſelf to *the deſires of the mind*, and doth not (as other kinds of writing, which are under the controul of *reaſon) buckle and bow the mind to the nature of things.*

But they, who like a principle the better for ſeeing it in Greek, may take it in the words of an old philoſopher, ERATOSTHENES, who affirmed — ποιητὴν πάντα στοχάζεσθαι ψυχαγωγίας, οὐ διδασκαλίας — of which words, the definition given above, is the tranſlation.

This *notion* of the end of poetry, if kept ſteadily in view, will unfold to us all the myſteries of the poetic art. There needs but to evolve the philoſopher's idea, and to apply it, as occaſion ſerves. *The art of poetry* will be, univerſally, THE ART OF PLEASING; and all its *rules*, but ſo many MEANS, which experience finds moſt conducive to that end;

Sic

Sic ANIMIS natum inventumque poëma JUVANDIS.

Ariſtotle has delivered and explained theſe rules, ſo far as they reſpect one ſpecies of poetry, the *dramatic*, or, more properly ſpeaking, the *tragic*: And when ſuch a writer, as he, ſhall do as much by the other ſpecies, then, and not till then, a complete ART OF POETRY will be formed.

I have not the preſumption to think myſelf, in any degree, equal to this arduous taſk: But from the idea of this art, as given above, an ordinary writer may undertake to deduce ſome general concluſions, concerning *Univerſal Poetry*, which ſeem preparatory to thoſe nicer diſquiſitions, concerning its *ſeveral ſorts or ſpecies*.

I. It follows from that IDEA, that it ſhould neglect no advantage, that fairly offers itſelf, of appearing in ſuch a dreſs or mode of language, as is moſt *taking* and agreeable to us. We may expect then, in the language or ſtyle of poetry, a choice of ſuch words as are moſt ſonorous and expreſſive, and ſuch an arrangement of them

them as throws the discourse out of the ordinary and common phrase of conversation. Novelty and variety are certain sources of pleasure: a construction of words, which is not vulgar, is therefore more suited to the ends of poetry, than one which we are every day accustomed to in familiar discourse. Some manners of placing them are, also, more agreeable to the ear, than others: Poetry, then, is studious of these, as it would by all means, not manifestly absurd, give pleasure: And hence a certain musical cadence, or what we call *Rhythm*, will be affected by the poet.

But, of all the means of adorning and enlivening a discourse by words, which are infinite, and perpetually grow upon us, as our knowledge of the tongue in which we write, and our skill in adapting it to the ends of poetry, increases, there is none that pleases more, than *figurative expression.*

By *figurative expression*, I would be understood to mean, here, that which respects *the pictures or images of things.* And this sort of figurative expression is universally

pleasing

pleasing to us, because it tends to impress on the mind the most distinct and vivid conceptions; and truth of representation being of less account in this way of composition, than the liveliness of it, poetry, as such, will delight in tropes and figures, and those the most strongly and forceably expressed. And though the *application* of figures will admit of great variety, according to the nature of the subject, and the *management* of them must be suited to the taste and apprehension of the people to whom they are addressed, yet, in some way or other, they will find a place in all works of poetry; and they who object to the use of them, only shew that they are not capable of being pleased by this sort of composition, or do, in effect, interdict the thing itself.

The antients looked for so much of this force and spirit of expression in whatever they dignified with the name of *poem*, that Horace tells us it was made a question by some, whether comedy were rightly referred to this class, because it differed only in point of measure from mere prose.

Idcirco

Idcirco quidam, comoedia necne poema
Effet, quaesivere: quod acer spiritus, ac vis,
Nec *verbis*, nec rebus inest: nisi quod pede certo
Differt sermoni, sermo merus— Sat. l. I. iv.

But they might have spared their doubt, or at least have resolved it, if they had considered that comedy adopts as much of this *force and spirit of words*, as is consistent with the *nature* and *degree* of that pleasure, which it pretends to give. For the name of poem will belong to every composition, whose primary end is to *please*, provided it be so constructed as to afford *all* the pleasure, which its kind or *sort* will permit.

II. From the idea of the *end* of poetry, it follows, that not only figurative and tropical terms will be employed in it, as *these*, by the images they convey, and by the air of novelty which such indirect ways of speaking carry with them, are found most delightful to us, but also that FICTION, in the largest sense of the word, is essential to poetry. For its purpose is, not to delineate truth simply, but to present it in the most taking forms; not to reflect the

real

real face of things, but to illuſtrate and adorn it; not to repreſent the faireſt objects only, but to repreſent them in the faireſt lights, and to heighten all their beauties up to the poſſibility of their natures; nay, to *outſtrip* nature, and to addreſs itſelf to our wildeſt fancy, rather than to our judgement and cooler ſenſe.

Οὔτ' ἐπιδερκτὰ τάδ' ἀνδράσιν, οὔτ' ἐπακουστὰ,
Οὔτε νόῳ περιληπτὰ—

as ſings one of the profeſſion [*a*], who ſeems to have underſtood his privileges very well.

For there is ſomething in the mind of man, ſublime and elevated, which prompts it to overlook all obvious and familiar appearances, and to feign to itſelf other and more extraordinary; ſuch as correſpond to the extent of its own powers, and fill out all the faculties and capacities of our ſouls. This reſtleſs and aſpiring diſpoſition, poetry, firſt and principally, would indulge and flatter; and thence takes its name of *divine*, as if ſome power, above

[*a*] Empedocles. See Plutarch, vol. i. p. 15. Par. 1624.

human,

human, conſpired. to lift the mind to theſe exalted conceptions.

Hence it comes to paſs, that it deals in apoſtrophes and invocations; that it impersonates the virtues and vices; peoples all creation with new and living forms; calls up infernal ſpectres to terrify, or brings down celeſtial natures to aſtoniſh, the imagination; aſſembles, combines, or connects its ideas, at pleaſure; in ſhort, prefers not only the agreeable and the graceful, but, as occaſion calls upon her, the vaſt, the incredible, I had almoſt ſaid, the impoſſible, to the obvious truth and nature of things. For all this is but a feeble expreſſion of that magic virtue of poetry, which our Shakeſpeare has ſo forcibly deſcribed in thoſe well-known lines —

The poet's eye, in a fine frenzy rowling,
Doth glance from heav'n to earth, from earth to heav'n;
And, as Imagination bodies forth
The forms of things unknown, the poet's pen
Turns them to ſhape, and gives to aery nothing
A local habitation and a name.

When

When the received syſtem of manners or religion in any country, happens to be ſo conſtituted as to ſuit itſelf in ſome degree to this extravagant turn of the human mind, we may expect that poetry will ſeize it with avidity, will dilate upon it with pleaſure, and take a pride to erect its ſpecious wonders on ſo proper and convenient a ground. Whence it cannot ſeem ſtrange that, of all the forms in which poetry has appeared, that of *pagan fable*, and *gothic romance*, ſhould, in their turns, be found the moſt alluring to the true poet. For, in defect of theſe advantages, he will ever adventure, in ſome ſort, to ſupply their place with others of his own invention; that is, he will mould every ſyſtem, and convert every ſubject, into the moſt amazing and miraculous form.

And this is that I would ſay, at preſent, of theſe two requiſites of univerſal poetry, namely, *that licence of expreſſion*, which we call the *ſtyle* of poetry, and *that licence of repreſentation*, which we call *fiction*. The *ſtyle* is, as it were, the body of poetry; *fiction*, is its ſoul. Having, thus, taken the privilege

privilege of a poet to create a Muse, we have only now to give her a voice, or more properly to *tune* it, and then she will be in a condition, as one of her favourites speaks, TO RAVISH ALL THE GODS. For

III. It follows from the same idea of the *end*; which poetry would accomplish, that not only Rhythm, but NUMBERS, properly so called, is essential to it. For this Art undertaking to gratify all those desires and expectations of pleasure, that can be reasonably entertained by us, and there being a capacity in language, the instrument it works by, of pleasing us very highly, not only by the sense and imagery it conveys, but by the structure of words, and still more by the harmonious arrangement of them in metrical sounds or numbers, and lastly there being no reason in the nature of the thing itself why these pleasures should not be united, it follows that poetry will not be that which it professes to be, that is, will not accomplish its own purpose, unless it delight the ear with numbers, or, in other words, unless it be cloathed in VERSE.

The reader, I dare ſay, has hitherto gone along with me, in this deduction: but here, I ſuſpect, we ſhall ſeparate. Yet he will ſtartle the leſs at this concluſion, if he reflect on the origin and firſt application of poetry among all nations.

It is every where of the moſt early growth, preceding every other ſort of compoſition; and being deſtined for the *ear*, that is, to be either ſung, or at leaſt recited, it adapts itſelf, even in its firſt rude eſſays, to that ſenſe of meaſure and proportion in ſounds, which is ſo natural to us. The hearer's attention is the ſooner gained by this means, his entertainment quickened, and his admiration of the performer's art excited. Men are ambitious of pleaſing, and ingenious in refining upon what they obſerve will pleaſe. So that muſical cadences and harmonious ſounds, which nature dictated, are farther ſoftened and improved by art, till poetry become as raviſhing to the ear, as the images, it preſents, are to the imagination. In proceſs of time, what was at firſt the extemporaneous production of genius or paſſion, under whose honour the great Geographer would assert, in his criticism on Eratosthenes) frequently *instruct us* by a true and faithful representation of things; yet even this instructive air is only assumed for the sake of *pleasing*; which, as the human mind is constituted, they could not so well do, if they did not instruct at all, that is, if *truth* were wholly neglected by them. So that *pleasure* is still the ultimate end and *scope* of the poet's art; and *instruction* itself is, in his hands, only one of the *means*, by which he would effect it [*b*].

I am the larger on this head, to shew that it is not a mere verbal dispute, as it is commonly thought, whether poems should be written in verse, or no. Men may include, or not include, the idea of metre in their complex idea of what they call a *Poem*. What I contend for, is, that *metre*, as an instrument of *pleasing*, is essential to every work of poetic art, and would therefore enter into such idea, if men judged of poetry according to its confessed *nature and end*.

[*b*] See STRABO, l. i. p. 15. Par. 1620.

Whence

Whence it may ſeem a little ſtrange, that my Lord Bacon ſhould ſpeak of *poeſy as a part of learning in meaſure of words* FOR THE MOST PART *reſtrained*; when his own notion, as we have ſeen above, was, that the eſſence of poetry conſiſted *in ſubmitting the ſhews of things to the deſires of the mind.* For theſe *ſhews of things* could only be exhibited to the mind through the *medium of words*: and it is juſt as natural for the mind to deſire that theſe words ſhould be *harmonious*, as that the images, conveyed in them, ſhould be *illuſtrious*; there being a capacity in the mind of being delighted through its organ, the *ear*, as well as through its power, or faculty of *imagination*. And the wonder is the greater, becauſe the great philoſopher himſelf was aware of *the agreement and conſort which poetry hath with muſic*, as well as *with man's nature and pleaſure*, that is, with the pleaſure which naturally reſults from gratifying the imagination. So that, to be conſiſtent with himſelf, he ſhould, methinks, have ſaid—*that poeſy was a part of learning in meaſure of words*

become a ſtanding law of the tragic ſtage. For this, as every other poem, being calculated and deſigned properly and ultimately to *pleaſe*, whatever contributes to produce that end moſt perfectly, all circumſtances taken into the account, muſt be thought of the nature or eſſence of the kind.

But, without carrying matters ſo far, let us confine our attention to metre, or what we call *verſe*. This muſt be eſſential to every work bearing the name of *poem*, not, becauſe we are only accuſtomed to call works written in verſe, *poems*, but becauſe a work, which profeſſes to pleaſe us by every poſſible and proper method, and yet does not give us this pleaſure, which it is in its power, and is no way improper for it, to give, muſt ſo far fall ſhort of fulfilling its own engagements to us; that is, it has not all thoſe qualities which we have a right to expect in a work of literary art, of which *pleaſure* is the ultimate *end*.

To explain myſelf by an obvious inſtance. Hiſtory undertakes to INSTRUCT us in the tranſactions of paſt times. If it anſwer

swer this purpose, it does all that is of *its nature*; and, if it find means to *please* us, besides, by the harmony of its style, and vivacity of its narration, all this is to be accounted as pure gain: if it instructed ONLY, by the truth of its reports, and the perspicuity of its method, it would fully attain its *end*. Poetry, on the other hand, undertakes to PLEASE. If it employ all its powers to this purpose, it effects all that is of *its nature*; if it serve, besides, to inform or instruct us, by the truths it conveys, and by the precepts or examples it inculcates, this service may rather be accepted, than required by us: if it pleased ONLY, by its ingenious fictions, and harmonious structure, it would discharge its office, and answer its *end*.

In this sense, the famous saying of Eratosthenes, quoted above—*that the poet's aim is to please, not to instruct*—is to be understood: nor does it appear, what reason Strabo could have to take offence at it; however it might be misapplied, as he tells us it was, by that writer. For, though the poets, no doubt (and especially THE POET, the conduct of a *natural ear*, becomes the labour of the closet, and is conducted by artificial rules; yet still, with a secret reference to the *sense* of hearing, and to that acceptation which melodious sounds meet with in the recital of expressive words.

Even the prose-writer (when the art is enough advanced to produce prose) having been accustomed to have his ear consulted and gratified by the poet, catches insensibly the same harmonious affection, tunes his sentences and periods to some agreement with song, and transfers into his coolest narrative, or gravest instruction, something of that music, with which his ear vibrates from poetic impressions.

In short, he leaves measured and determinate numbers, that is, METRE, to the poet, who is to please up to the height of his faculties, and the nature of his work; and only reserves to himself, whose purpose of giving pleasure is subordinate to another end, the looser musical measure, or what we call RHYTHMICAL PROSE.

The reason appears, from this deduction, why *all* poetry aspires to please by melo-

dious

dious numbers. To *some* species it is thought more essential, than to others, because those species continue to be *sung*, that is, are more immediately addressed to the ear; and because they continue to be sung in concert with *musical instruments*, by which the ear is still more indulged. It happened in antient Greece, that even tragedy retained this accompaniment of musical instruments, through all its stages, and even in its most improved state. Whence Aristotle includes *music*, properly so called, as well as *Rhythm* and *Metre*, in his idea of the tragic poem. He did this, because he found the drama of his country, OMNIBUS NUMERIS ABSOLUTUM, I mean in possession of all the advantages which could result from the union of *rhythmical*, *metrical*, and *musical* sounds. Modern tragedy has relinquished part of these: yet still, if it be true that this poem be more pleasing by the addition of the *musical* art, and there be nothing in the nature of the composition which forbids the use of it, I know not why Aristotle's idea should not be adopted, and his precept

 become

ALWAYS *restrained*; such *poesy*, as, through the idleness or negligence of writers, is not so restrained, not agreeing to his own idea of *this part of learning* [c].

These reflexions will afford a proper solution of that question, which has been agitated by the critics, "Whether a work "of fiction and imagination (such as that "of the archbishop of Cambray, for in-"stance) conducted, in other respects, ac-"cording to the rules of the epic poem, but "written in prose, may deserve the name of "POEM, or not." For, though it be frivolous indeed to dispute about names, yet from what has been said it appears, that if metre be not incongruous to the nature of an epic-composition, and it afford a pleasure which is not to be found in mere prose, metre is, for that reason, essential to this mode of writing; which is only saying in other words, that an epic composition, to give all the pleasure which it is capable of giving, must be written in *verse*.

[c] ADV. OF LEARNING, vol. i. p. 50. Dr Birch's Ed. 1765.

But,

But, secondly, this conclusion, I think, extends farther than to such works as aspire to the name of *epic*. For instance, what are we to think of those *novels* or *romances*, as they are called; that is, fables constructed on some private and familiar subject, which have been so current, of late, through all Europe? As they propose *pleasure* for their end, and prosecute it, besides, in the way of *fiction*, though without metrical numbers, and generally, indeed, in harsh and rugged prose, one easily sees what their pretensions are, and under what idea they are ambitious to be received. Yet, as they are wholly destitute of measured sounds (to say nothing of their other numberless defects) they can, at most, be considered but as hasty, imperfect, and abortive poems; whether spawned from the dramatic, or narrative species, it may be hard to say —

> Unfinish'd things, one knows not what to call,
> Their generation's so equivocal.

However, such as they are, these *novelties* have been generally well received: *Some*, for the real merit of their execution;

Others,

ful and harmonious than the French, may afford all the melody of ſound which is expected in ſome ſorts of poetry, by its *varied pauſe*, and *quantity* only; while in other ſorts, which are more ſollicitous to pleaſe the ear, and where ſuch ſollicitude, if taken notice of by the reader or hearer, is not reſented, it may be proper, or rather it becomes a law of the Engliſh and Italian poetry, to adopt *rhyme*. Thus, our tragedies are uſually compoſed in blank verſe: but our epic and lyric compoſitions are found moſt pleaſing, when cloathed in rhyme. Milton, I know, it will be ſaid, is an exception: But, if we ſet aſide ſome learned perſons, who have ſuffered themſelves to be too eaſily prejudiced by their admiration of the Greek and Latin languages, and ſtill more, perhaps, by the prevailing notion of the monkiſh or gothic original of rhymed verſe, all other readers, if left to themſelves, would, I dare ſay, be more delighted with this poet, if, beſides his various pauſe, and meaſured quantity, he had enriched his numbers, with *rhyme*. So that his love of liberty, the ruling paſ-

ſion

ſion of his heart, perhaps tranſported him too far, when he choſe to follow the example ſet him by one or two writers of *prime note* (to uſe his own eulogium), rather than comply with the regular and prevailing practice of his favoured Italy, which firſt and principally, as our beſt rhymiſt ſings,

> With pauſes, cadence, and well-vowell'd words,
> And all the graces a good ear affords,
> MADE RHYME AN ART—

Our comedy, indeed, is generally written in *proſe*; but through the idleneſs, or ill taſte, of our writers, rather than from any other juſt cauſe. For, though rhyme be not neceſſary, or rather would be improper, in the comedy of our language, which can ſupport itſelf in poetic numbers, without the diligence of rhyme; yet ſome ſort of metre is requiſite in this humbler ſpecies of poem; otherwiſe, it will not contribute all that is within its power and province, to *pleaſe*. And the particular metre, proper for this ſpecies, is not far to ſeek. For it can plainly be no other than a careleſs and looſer Iambic, ſuch as our language naturally are ſtudiouſly avoided by good writers; while in others, as in all the modern ones, where theſe conſonances are leſs frequent, and where the quantity of ſyllables is not ſo diſtinctly marked as, of itſelf, to afford an harmonious meaſure and muſical variety, there it is of neceſſity that poets have had recourſe to *Rhyme*; or to ſome other expedient of the like nature, ſuch as the *Alliteration*, for inſtance; which is only another way of delighting the ear by iterated ſound, and may be defined, *the conſonance of initial letters*, as rhyme is, the *conſonance of final ſyllables*. All this, I ſay, is of neceſſity, becauſe what we call verſes in ſuch languages will be otherwiſe untuneful, and will not ſtrike the ear with that vivacity, which is requiſite to put a ſenſible difference between poetic numbers and meaſured proſe.

In ſhort, no method of gratifying the ear by *meaſured ſound*, which experience has found pleaſing, is to be neglected by the poet: and although, from the different ſtructure and genius of languages, theſe methods will be different, the ſtudious

application

application of such methods, as each particular language allows, becomes a necessary part of his office. He will only cultivate those methods most, which tend to produce, in a given language, the most harmonious structure or measure, of which it is capable.

Hence it comes to pass, that the poetry of some modern languages cannot so much as subsist, without rhyme: In others, it is only embellished by it. Of the *former* sort is the French, which therefore adopts, and with good reason, rhymed verse, not in tragedy only, but in comedy: And though foreigners, who have a language differently constructed, are apt to treat this observance of rhyme as an idle affectation, yet it is but just to allow that the French themselves are the most competent judges of the natural defect of their own tongue, and the likeliest to perceive by what management such defect is best remedied or concealed.

In the *latter* class of languages, whose poetry is only embellished by the use of rhyme, we may reckon the Italian and the English: which being naturally more tuneful

Others, for their amuſing ſubjects; *All* of them, for the gratification they afford, or promiſe at leaſt, to a vitiated, palled, and ſickly imagination—that laſt diſeaſe of learned minds, and ſure prognoſtic of expiring Letters. But whatever may be the temporary ſucceſs of theſe things (for they vaniſh as faſt as they are produced, and are produced as ſoon as they are conceived) good ſenſe will acknowledge no work of art but ſuch as is compoſed according to the laws of its *kind*. Theſe KINDS, as arbitrary things as we account them (for I neither forget nor diſpute what our beſt philoſophy teaches concerning *kinds* and *ſorts*), have yet ſo far their foundation in nature and the reaſon of things, that it will not be allowed us to multiply, or vary them, at pleaſure. We may, indeed, mix and confound them, if we will (for there is a ſort of literary luxury, which would engroſs all pleaſures at once, even ſuch as are contradictory to each other), or, in our rage for inceſſant gratification, we may take up with half-formed pleaſures, ſuch as come firſt to hand, and

may

may be adminiftered by any body: But true tafte requires chafte, fevere, and fimple pleafures; and true genius will only be concerned in adminiftering fuch.

Laftly, on the fame principle on which we have decided on thefe queftions concerning the *abfolute merits* of poems in profe, in *all* languages, we may, alfo, determine another, which has been put concerning the *comparative merits* of RHYMED, and what is called BLANK verfe, in our *own*, and the other *modern* languages.

Critics and antiquaries have been follicitous to find out who were the inventors of rhyme, which fome fetch from the Monks, fome from the Goths, and others from the Arabians: whereas, the truth feems to be, that *rhyme*, or the confonance of final fyllables, occurring at fixed intervals, is the dictate of nature, or, as we may fay, an appeal to the *ear*, in all languages, and in fome degree pleafing in all. The difference is, that, in fome languages, thefe confonances are apt of themfelves to occur fo often that they rather naufeate, than pleafe, and fo, inftead of being affected,

are

naturally runs into, even in converſation, and of which we are not without examples, in our old and beſt writers for the comic ſtage. But it is not wonderful that thoſe critics, who take offence at Engliſh epic poems in *rhyme*, becauſe the Greek and Latin only obſerved *quantity*, ſhould require Engliſh comedies to be written in *proſe*, though the Greek and Latin comedies were compoſed in *verſe*. For the ill application of examples, and the neglect of them, may be well enough expected from the ſame men, ſince it does not appear that their judgment was employed, or the reaſon of the thing attended to, in either inſtance.

AND THUS much for the idea of UNIVERSAL POETRY. It is the art of treating any ſubject in *ſuch* a way as is found moſt delightful to us; that is, IN AN ORNAMENTED AND NUMEROUS STYLE — IN THE WAY OF FICTION — AND IN VERSE. Whatever deſerves the name of POEM muſt unite theſe three properties; only in different degrees of each, according to its nature. For the art of every *kind* of poetry

poetry is only this general art ſo modified as the *nature* of each, that is, its more immediate and ſubordinate end, may reſpectively require.

We are now, then, at the well-head of the poetic art; and they who drink deeply of this ſpring, will be beſt qualified to perform the reſt. But all heads are not equal to theſe copious draughts; and, beſides, I hear the ſober reader admoniſhing me long ſince—

Luſiſti ſatis atque BIBISTI;
Tempus abire tibi eſt, ne POTUM LARGIUS AEQUO
Rideat, et pulſet laſciva decentius AETAS.

THURCASTON,
MDCCLXV.

DISSERTATION II.

ON

THE PROVINCES OF THE DRAMA.

IN the former Essay, I gave an idea, or slight sketch, of *Universal Poetry*. In this, I attempt to deduce the laws of one of its kinds, the *Dramatic*, under all its forms. And I engage in this task, the rather, because, though much has been said on the subject of the drama, writers seem not to have taken sufficient pains to distinguish, with exactness, its several species.

I deduce the laws of this poem, as I did those of poetry at large, from the consideration of its *end*: not the general end of poetry, which alone was proper to be considered in the former case, but the proximate end of this kind. For from these ends, in subordination to that, which governs the genus, or which all poetry, as ſuch, deſigns and proſecutes, are the peculiar rules and maxims of each ſpecies to be derived.

THE PURPOSE OF THE DRAMA is, univerſally, "to repreſent human life in the "way of *action*." But as ſuch repreſentation is made for ſeparate and diſtinct ENDS, it is, further, diſtinguiſhed into different *ſpecies*, which we know by the names of TRAGEDY, COMEDY, and FARCE.

By TRAGEDY, then, I mean that ſpecies of dramatic repreſentation, whoſe *end* is "*to excite the paſſions of* PITY *and* TERROR, *and perhaps ſome others, nearly allied to them.*"

By COMEDY *that*, which propoſeth, for the *ends* of its repreſentation, "*the ſenſation of pleaſure ariſing from a view of the truth of* CHARACTERS, *more eſpecially their ſpecific differences.*"

By FARCE I underſtand that ſpecies of the drama, "*whoſe ſole aim and tendency is to excite* LAUGHTER."

The idea of theſe *three ſpecies* being then propoſed, let us now ſee, what concluſions may be drawn from it. And chiefly in respect of *Tragedy* and *Comedy*, which are most important. For as to what concerns the province of *Farce*, this will be easily understood, when the character of the other two is once settled.

CHAP. I.

ON THE PROVINCES OF TRAGEDY AND COMEDY.

FROM the idea of these two species, as given above, the following conclusions, about the *natures* of each are immediately deducible.

1. If the proper end of TRAGEDY be to *affect*, it follows, "that *actions*, not characters, are the chief object of its representations." For that which *affects* us most in the view of human life is the observation of those signal circumstances of *felicity or distress*, which occur in the fortunes of men. But *felicity* and *distress*, as the great critic takes notice, depend on *action*; κατὰ τὰς πράξεις, εὐδαίμονες, ἢ τοὐναντίον. They are then the calamitous *events*, or fortunate *issues* in human action, which stir up the stronger *affections*, and agitate the

 heart

heart with *Paſſion*. The *manners* are not, indeed, to be neglected. But they become an inferior conſideration in the views of the tragic poet, and are exhibited only for the ſake of making the *action* more proper to intereſt us. Thus our *joy* on the *happy cataſtrophe* of the fable, depends, in a good degree, on the *virtuous character* of the agent; as, on the other hand, we ſympathize more ſtrongly with him, on a *diſtreſsful iſſue*. The *manners* of the ſeveral perſons in the drama muſt, alſo, be ſignified, that the *action*, which in many caſes will be determined by them, may appear to be carried on with *truth and probability*. Hence every thing paſſing before us, as we are accuſtomed to ſee it in real life, we enter more warmly into their intereſts, as forgetting, that we are attentive to a *fictitious ſcene*. And, beſides, from knowing the perſonal *good or ill qualities* of the agents, we learn to anticipate their future *felicity* or *miſery*, which gives increaſe to the *paſſion* in either caſe. Our acquaintance with Iago's *cloſe villainy* makes us tremble for Othello and Deſdemona beforehand: and

HAMLET's *filial piety and intrepid daring* occasion the audience secretly to exult in the *expectation* of some successful vengeance to be inflicted on the incestuous murderers.

2. For the same reason as tragedy takes for its *object* the actions of men, it, also, prefers, or rather confines itself to, such actions, as are most *important*. Which is only saying, that as it intends to *interest*, it, of course, chuses the representation of those *events*, which are most *interesting*.

And this shews the defect of modern tragedy, in turning so constantly as it does, on *love subjects*; the effect of this practice is, that, excepting only the rank of the actors (which indeed, as will be seen presently, is of considerable importance), the rest is below the dignity of this drama. For the *action*, when stripped of its accidental ornaments and reduced to the *essential fact*, is nothing more than what might as well have passed in a cottage, as a king's palace. The Greek poets should be our guides here, who take the very grandest events in their story to ennoble their tragedy. Whence it comes to paſs that the *action*, having an eſſential dignity, is always *intereſting*, and by the ſimpleſt management of the poet becomes in a ſupreme degree, *pathetic*.

3. On the ſame account, the *perſons*, whoſe actions Tragedy would exhibit to us, muſt be of *principal rank and dignity*. For the actions of theſe are, both in *themſelves* and in their *conſequences*, moſt fitted to excite paſſion. The *diſtreſſes* of private and inferior perſons will, no doubt, *affect* us greatly; and we may give the name of *tragedies*, if we pleaſe, to dramatic repreſentations of them: as, in fact, we have ſeveral applauded pieces of this kind. Nay, it may ſeem, that the fortunes of private men, as more nearly reſembling *thoſe* of the generality, ſhould be moſt *affecting*. But this circumſtance in no degree makes amends for the loſs of other and much greater *advantages*. For, whatever be the *unhappy incidents* in the ſtory of private men, it is certain, they muſt take faſter hold of the *imagination*, and, of courſe, impreſs the heart more forcibly, when related

lated of the higher characters in life.

> Τῶν γὰρ μεγάλων ἀξιοπενθεῖς
> Φῆμαι μᾶλλον κατέχουσι.
>
> EURIP. HIPP. 1484.

Kings, Heroes, Statesmen, and other persons of great and public authority, influence by their *ill-fortune* the whole community, to which they belong. The attention is rouzed, and all our faculties take an alarm, at the apprehension of such extensive and important wretchedness. And, besides, if we regard the *event* itself, without an eye to its *effects*, there is still the widest difference between the two cases. Those ideas of awe and veneration, which opinion throws round the persons of princes, make us esteem the very *same event* in their fortunes, as more august and emphatical, than in the fortunes of private men. In the *one*, it is ordinary and familiar to our conceptions; it is singular and surprizing, in the *other*. The fall of a *cottage*, by the accidents of time and weather, is almost unheeded; while the ruin of a *tower*, which the neighbourhood hath gazed at, for ages, with

with admiration, ſtrikes all obſervers with concern. So that, if we chuſe to continue the abſurdity, taken notice of in the laſt article, of planning *unimportant action* in our tragedy, we ſhould, at leaſt, take care to give it this foreign and extrinſic *importance* of great *actors*: Yet our paſſion for the *familiar* goes ſo far, that we have tragedies, not only of private action, but of *private perſons*; and ſo have well nigh annihilated the nobleſt of the two dramas amongſt us. On the whole it appears, that as the proper object of tragedy is *action*, ſo it is *important* action, and therefore more eſpecially the action of *great and illuſtrious men*. Each of theſe concluſions is the direct conſequence of our idea of its *end*.

The reverſe of all this holds true of COMEDY. For,

1. Comedy, by the very terms of the definition, is converſant about *characters*. And, if we obſerve, that which creates the pleaſure we find in contemplating the lives of men, conſidered as diſtinct from the *intereſt* we take in their fortunes, is the contemplation

templation of their manners and humours. Their *actions*, when they are not of that sort, which seizes our admiration, or catches the affections, are no otherwise considered by us, than as they are sensible indications of the internal sentiment and disposition. Our intimate consciousness of the several turns and windings of our nature, makes us attend to these pictures of human life with an incredible curiosity. And herein the proper entertainment, which comic representation, *as such*, administers to the mind, consists. By turning the thought on *event and action*, this entertainment is proportionably lessened; that is, the *end* of comedy is less perfectly attained [d].

[d] Aristotle was of the same mind, as appears from his definition of comedy, which, says he, is ΜΙΜΗΣΙΣ ΦΑΥΛΟΤΕΡΩΝ. [κ. έ.] that is, *the imitation of characters*, whatever be the distinct meaning of the term φαυλότεροι. It is true, this critic, in his account of the origin of tragedy and comedy, makes them both the imitations of ACTIONS. Οἱ μὲν σεμνότεροι ΤΑΣ ΚΑΛΑΣ ἐμιμοῦντο ΠΡΑΞΕΙΣ, οἱ δὲ εὐτελέστεροι ΤΑΣ τῶν φαύλων. [κ. δ.] Yet, even here, the expression is so put, as if he had been conscious that *persons*, not *actions*, were the direct object of comedy. And the quotation, now alledged from another place, where

But-

But here, again, though *action* be not the main object of comedy, yet it is not to be neglected, any more than *character* in tragedy, but comes in as an useful accessary, or assistant to it. For the *manners of men* only shew themselves, or shew themselves most usually, in *action*. It is this, which fetches out the latent strokes of *character*, and renders the inward *temper and disposition* the object of sense. *Probable circumstances* are then imagined, and a certain *train of action* contrived, to evidence the *internal qualities*. There is no *other*, or no *probable* way, but this, of bringing us acquainted with them. Again; by engaging his *characters* in a course of action and the pursuit of some *end*, the comic poet leaves them to express themselves undisguisedly, and *without design*; in which the essence of *humour* consists.

Add to this, that when the *fable* is so contrived as to attach the mind, we very naturally fancy ourselves present at a course of *living* action. And this illusion quickens

a definition is given more in form, shews, that this was, in effect, his sentiment.

our attention to the *characters*, which no longer appear to us creatures of the poet's fiction, but actors in real life.

These observations concerning the *moderated* use of action in comedy, instruct us what to think "of those intricate Spanish "plots, which have been in use, and have "taken both with us and some French "writers for the stage. The truth is, "they have hindered very much the main "end of comedy. For when these un"natural plots are used, the mind is not "only entirely *drawn off* from the cha"racters by those surprizing turns and re"volutions; but characters have no oppor"tunity even of being *called out* and dis"playing themselves. For the actors of all "characters *succeed* and are *embarrassed* "alike, when the instruments for carrying "on designs are only *perplexed apartments*, "*dark entries*, *disguised habits*, and *ladders* "*of ropes*. The comic plot is, and must, "indeed, be carried on by *deceipt*. The "Spanish scene does it by deceiving the "man *through his senses*: Terence and Mo"liere, by deceiving him *through his passions*

"*and*

"*and affections.* This is the right method: "for the character is *not* called out under "the *first* species of deceipt: under the "*second*, the character does *all.*"

2. As *character*, not *action*, is the object of comedy; so the *characters* it paints must not be of *singular and illustrious note*, either for their *virtues* or *vices*. The reason is, that such characters take too fast hold of the *affections*, and so call off the mind from adverting to the *truth* of the manners; that is, from receiving the *pleasure*, which this poem *intends*. Our *sense of imitation* is that to which the comic poet addresses himself; but such pictures of *eminent worth* or *villainy* seize upon the *moral sense*; and by raising the strong correspondent passions of *admiration* and *abhorrence*, turn us aside from contemplating the *imitation itself*. And,

3. For a like cause, comedy confines its views to the characters of *private and inferior persons*. For the *truth of character*, which is the spring of *humour*, being necessarily, as was observed, to be shewn through the medium of *action*, and the actions

actions of the great being usually such as excite the *pathos*, it follows of course, that these cannot, with propriety, be made the actors in comedy. Persons of high and public life, if they are drawn agreeably to our accustomed ideas of them, must be employed in such a *course of action*, as arrests the attention, or interests the passions; and either way it diverts the mind from observing the *truth* of manners, that is, it prevents the attainment of the specific *end*, which comedy designs.

And if the reason, here given, be sufficient to exclude the *higher characters* in life from this *drama*, even where the representation is intended to be *serious*, we shall find it still more improper to expose them in any pleasant or ridiculous light. It is true, the follies and foibles of the great will apparently take an easier ridicule by representation, than those of their inferiors. And this it was, which misled the celebrated P. CORNEILLE into the opinion, *that the actions of the great, and even of kings themselves, provided they be of the ridiculous kind, are as fit objects of comedy, as any*

any other. But he did not reflect, that the *actions* of the great being usually such, as interest the intire community, at least scarcely any other falling beneath vulgar notice; and the higher *characters* being rarely seen or contemplated by the people but with reverence, hence it is, that in fact, *the representation of high life* cannot, without offence to probability, be made *ridiculous*, or consequently be admitted into comedy under this view. And therefore PLAUTUS, when he thought fit to introduce these *reverend personages* on the comic stage in his AMPHITRUO, though he employed them in no very serious matters, was yet obliged to apologize for this impropriety in calling his play a *Tragi-comedy*. What he says upon the occasion, though delivered with an air of pleasantry, is, according to the laws of just criticism:

> *Faciam ut commista sit* TRAGICO-COMOEDIA.
> *Nam me perpetuo facere, ut sit Comoedia,*
> REGES QUO VENIANT ET DII, *non par arbitror.*
> *Quid igitur? quoniam hic* SERVOS QUOQUE PARTES HABET,
> *Faciam sit, proinde ut dixi,* TRAGICO-COMEDIA.
>
> PROL. IN AMPHIT.

And

And now, taking the *idea* of the *two dramas*, as here opened, along with us, we shall be able to give an account of several attributes, *common* to both, or which further *characterize* each of them. And,

1. *A plot will be required in both.* For the end of tragedy being to excite the affections *by* action; and the end of comedy, to manifest the truth of character *through* it; an artful *constitution of the Fable* is required to do justice both to the one and the other. It serves to bring out the *pathos*, and to produce *humour*. And thus the general form or structure of the two dramas will be one and the same.

2. More particularly, *an unity and even simplicity in the conduct of the fable* [e] *is a*

[e] The neglect of this is one of the greatest defects in the *modern drama*; which in nothing falls so much short of the perfection of the Greek scene as in this want of simplicity in the construction of its fable. The good sense of the author of the *History of the Italian Theatre* (who, though a mere player, appears to have had juster notions of the drama, than the generality of even professed critics) was sensibly struck with this difference in *tragedy*. "Quant à "l'unité d'action," says he, "je trouve une grande dif-"ference entre les tragedies Grecques et les trage-

perfection in each. For the course of the *affections* is diverted and weakened by the intervention of what we call a *double plot*; and even by a multiplicity of *subordinate events*, though tending to a common *end*; and of *persons*, though all of them, some way, concerned in promoting it. The like consideration shews the observance of this *rule* to be essential to just comedy. For when the *attention* is split on so many interfering objects, we are not at leisure to observe, nor do we so fully enter into, the *truth of representation* in any of them; the *sense* of *humour*, as of the *pathos*, depending very much on the continued and undiverted operation of its *object* upon us.

3. The two dramas agree, also, in this circumstance; that the *manners* of the persons exhibited should be *imperfect*. An absolutely *good*, or an absolutely *bad*, cha-

"dies Françoises; j'apperçois toûjours aisément "l'action des tragedies Grecques, et je ne la perds "point de vûe; mais dans les tragedies Françoises, "j'avoüe, que j'ai souvent bien de la peine à demêler "l'action des episodes, dont elle est chargée." [*Hist. du Theatre Italien, par* LOUIS RICCOBONI, p. 293. *Paris*, 1728.]

racter

racter is foreign to the purpose of each. And the reason is, 1. That such a representation is *improbable*. And *probability* constitutes, as we have seen, the very essence of comedy; and is the *medium*, through which tragedy is enabled most powerfully to affect us. 2. Such *characters* are improper to *comedy*, because, as was hinted above, they turn the attention aside from contemplating the *expression* of them, which we call *humour*. And they are not less unsuited to *tragedy*, because though they make a forcible impression on the mind, yet, as Aristotle well observes, they do not produce the passions of *pity and terror*; that is, their *impressions* are not of the nature of that *pathos*, by which tragedy works its purpose. [z. 17].

There are, likewise, some peculiarities, which distinguish the two dramas. And

1. *Though a plot be necessary to produce* humour, *as well as the pathos*; *yet a* good plot *is not so essential to comedy, as tragedy*. For the pathos is the result of the *entire action*, that is, of all the circumstances of the story taken together, and conspiring, by

a probable tendency, to a completion in the *event*. A failure in the just arrangement and disposition of the parts may, then, affect what is of the essence of this drama. On the contrary, *humour*, though brought out by *action*, is not the effect of the *whole*, but may be distinctly evidenced in a *single scene*; as may be eminently illustrated in the two comedies of Fletcher, called *The Little French Lawyer*, and *The Spanish Curate*. The nice contexture of the fable, therefore, though it may give a *pleasure* of another kind, is not so immediately required to the production of *that* pleasure, which the nature of comedy demands. Much less is there occasion for that labour and ingenuity of contrivance, which is seen in the intricacy of the Spanish fable. Yet this is the taste of our comedy. Our writers are all for plot and intrigue; and never appear so well satisfied with themselves as when, to speak in their own phrase, they contrive to have a great deal of *business* on their hands. Indeed they have reason. For it hides their inability to colour *man-*

ners,

ners, which is the proper but much harder province of true comedy.

2. *Tragedy ſucceeds beſt, when the ſubject is* real; *comedy, when it is* feigned. What would this ſay, but that tragedy, turning our attention principally on the *action repreſented*, finds means to *intereſt* us more ſtrongly on the perſuaſion of its being taken from *actual life?* While comedy, on the other hand, can neglect theſe ſcrupulous meaſures of *probability*, as intent only on exhibiting *characters*; for which purpoſe an *invented ſtory* will ſerve much better. The reaſon is, *real action* does not ordinarily afford variety of incidents enough to ſhew the *character* fully: *feigned action* may.

And this difference, we may obſerve, explains the reaſon why tragedies are often formed on the moſt *trite and vulgar ſubjects*, whereas a *new* ſubject is generally demanded in comedy. The *reality* of the ſtory being of ſo much conſequence to intereſt the affections, the more *known* it is, the fitter for the poet's purpoſe. But a *feigned* ſtory having been found more convenient for the display of characters, it grew into a rule that the story should be always *new*. This disadvantage on the side of the comic poet is taken notice of in those verses of Antiphanes, or rather, as Casaubon conjectures, of *Aristophanes*, in a play of his, intitled, Ποίησις. The reason of this difference now appears.

—Μακάριόν ἐστιν ἡ τραγῳδία
Ποίημα κατὰ πάντ'. εἴγε πρῶτον οἱ λόγοι
Ὑπὸ τῶν θεατῶν εἰσὶν ἐγνωρισμένοι,
Πρὶν καί τιν' εἰπεῖν, ὡς ὑπομνῆσαι μόνον
Δεῖ τὸν ποιητήν· Οἰδίπουν γὰρ ἄν γε φῶ,
Τὰ δ' ἄλλα πάντ' ἴσασιν. Ὁ πατὴρ Λάϊος
Μήτηρ Ἰοκάστη, θυγατέρες, παῖδες, τίνες·
Τί πείσεθ' οὗτος, τί πεποίηκεν····
Ἡμῖν δὲ ταῦτ' οὐκ ἔστιν· ἀλλὰ πάντα δεῖ
Εὑρεῖν ὀνόματα καινὰ, τὰ διῳκημένα
Πρότερον, τὰ νῦν παρόντα, τὴν καταστροφὴν,
Τὴν ἐσβολήν. ἂν ἕν τι τούτων παραλίπῃ,
Χρέμης τις, ἢ Φείδων τις ἐκσυρίττεται,
Πηλεῖ δὲ ταῦτ' ἔξεστι καὶ Τεύκρῳ ποιεῖν.

One sees, then, the reason why Tragedy prefers real *subjects*, and even old ones; and,

and, on the contrary, why comedy delights in feigned ſubjects, and new.

The ſame genius in the two dramas is obſervable, in their draught of *characters*. Comedy makes all its Characters *general*; Tragedy, *particular*. The *Avare* of Moliere is not ſo properly the picture of a *covetous man*, as of *covetouſneſs* itſelf. Racine's *Nero*, on the other hand, is not a picture of *cruelty*, but of a *cruel man*.

Yet here it will be proper to guard againſt two miſtakes, which the principles now delivered may be thought to countenance.

The *firſt* is with regard to *tragic* characters, which I ſay are *particular*. My meaning is, they are *more* particular than thoſe of comedy. That is, the *end* of tragedy does not require or permit the poet to draw together ſo many of thoſe characteriſtic circumſtances which ſhew the manners, as Comedy. For, in the former of theſe dramas, no more of *character* is ſhewn, than what the courſe of the action neceſſarily calls forth. Whereas, all or moſt of the features, by which it is uſually diſtinguiſhed, are ſought out and induſtriouſly diſplayed in the *latter*.

The caſe is much the ſame as in *portrait painting*; where, if a great maſter be required to draw a *particular face*, he gives the very lineaments he finds in it; yet ſo far reſembling to what he obſerves of the ſame turn in other faces, as not to affect any minute circumſtance of peculiarity. But if the ſame artiſt were to deſign a *head* in general, he would aſſemble together all the cuſtomary traits and features, any where obſervable through the ſpecies, which ſhould beſt expreſs the idea, whatever it was, he had conceived in his own mind, and wanted to exhibit in the picture.

There is much the ſame difference between the two ſorts of *dramatic* portraits. Whence it appears that in calling the tragic character *particular*, I ſuppoſe it only *leſs repreſentative* of the kind than the comic; not that the draught of ſo much character as it is concerned to repreſent ſhould not be *general*: the contrary of which I have aſſerted and explained at large elſeweere [*Notes on the A. P.* 317.]

Next,

Next, I have ſaid, the characters of juſt comedy are *general*. And this I explain by the inſtance of the *Avare* of Moliere, which conforms more to the idea of *avarice*, than to that of the real *avaricious man*. But here again, the reader will not underſtand me, as ſaying this in the ſtrict ſenſe of the words. I even think Moliere faulty in the inſtance given; though, with ſome neceſſary explanation, it may well enough ſerve to expreſs my meaning.

The view of the comic ſcene being to delineate characters, this end, I ſuppoſe, will be attained moſt perfectly, by making thoſe characters as *univerſal* as poſſible. For thus the perſon ſhewn in the drama, being the repreſentative of all characters of the ſame kind, furniſhes in the higheſt degree the entertainment of *humour*. But then this univerſality muſt be ſuch as agrees not to our idea of the *poſſible* effects of the character as conceived in the abſtract, but to the *actual* exertion of its powers; which experience juſtifies, and common life allows. Moliere, and before him Plautus, had offended in this; that for a picture of the *avaritious man*, they presented us with a fantastic unpleasing draught of the *passion of avarice*. I call this a *fantastic* draught, because it hath no archetype in nature. And it is, farther, an *unpleasing* one; for, being the delineation of a *simple passion unmixed*, it wanted all those

—Lights and shades, whose well-accorded strife
Gives all the strength and colour of our life.

These *lights and shades* (as the poet finely calls the intermixture of many passions, which, with the *leading* or principal one, form the human character) must be blended together in every picture of dramatic manners; because the avowed business of the drama is to image real life. Yet the draught of the *leading* passion must be as general as this *strife* in nature permits, in order to express the intended character more perfectly.

All which again is easily illustrated in the instance of painting. In *portraits of character*, as we may call those that give a picture of the *manners*, the artist, if he be of real ability, will not go to work on the possibility

poſſibility of an abſtract idea. All he intends is, to ſhew that ſome one quality *predominates*: and this he images ſtrongly, and by ſuch ſignatures as are moſt conſpicuous in the operation of the *leading paſſion*. And when he hath done this, we may, in common ſpeech or in compliment, if we pleaſe, to his art, ſay of ſuch a portrait that it images to us not the *man*, but the *paſſion*; juſt as the antients obſerved of the famous ſtatue of Apollodorus by Silarion, that it expreſſed not the angry *Apollodorous*, but his paſſion of *anger* [*f*]. But by this muſt be underſtood only that he has well expreſſed the leading parts of the deſigned character. For the reſt, he treats his *ſubject* as he would any other; that is, he repreſents the *concomitant affections*, or conſiders merely that general ſymmetry and proportion which are expected in a human figure. And this is to copy nature, which affords no ſpecimen of a man turned all into a ſingle paſſion. No metamorphoſis could be more ſtrange or incredible.

[*f*] *Non hominem ex ære fecit, ſed iracundiam.* Plin. xxxiv. 8.

Yet portraits of this vicious taste are the admiration of common starers, who, if they find a picture of a *miser* for instance (as there is no commoner subject of moral portraits) in a collection, where every muscle is strained, and feature hardened into the expression of this idea, never fail to profess their wonder and approbation of it.—On this idea of excellence, Le Brun's book of the PASSIONS must be said to contain a set of the justest *moral portraits*: And the CHARACTERS of Theophrastus might be recommended, in a *dramatic* view, as preferable to those of Terence.

The virtuosi in the fine arts would certainly laugh at the former of these judgments. But the latter, I suspect, will not be thought so extraordinary: at least if one may guess from the practice of some of our best comic writers, and the success which such plays have commonly met with. It were easy to instance in almost all plays of character. But if the reader would see the extravagance of building dramatic manners on abstract ideas, in its full light, he needs only turn to B. Jonson's *Every man out of his humour*; which, under the name of a *play of character*, is in fact an unnatural, and, as the painters call it, *hard* delineation of a group of *simply existing passions*, wholly chimerical, and unlike to any thing we observe in the commerce of real life. Yet this comedy has always had its admirers. And *Randolph*, in particular, was so taken with the design, that he seems to have formed his *muse's looking-glass* in express imitation of it.

Shakespeare, we may observe, is in this, as in all the other more essential beauties of the drama, a perfect model. If the discerning reader peruse attentively his comedies with this view, he will find his *best-marked* characters discoursing, through a great deal of their *parts*, just like any other, and only expressing their essential and leading qualities occasionally, and as circumstances concur to give an easy exposition to them. This singular excellence of his comedy, was the effect of his copying faithfully after nature, and of the force and vivacity of his genius, which made him attentive to what the progress of the scene successively

ceſſively preſented to him: whilſt *imitation* and *inferior talents* occaſion little writers to wind themſelves up into the habit of attending perpetually to their main view, and a ſolicitude to keep their favourite characters in conſtant play and agitation. Though, in this illiberal exerciſe of their wit, they may be ſaid to uſe the *perſons of their drama* as a certain facetious ſort do their *acquaintance*, whom they urge and teize with their civilities, not to give them a reaſonable ſhare in the converſation, but to force them to play *tricks* for the diverſion of the company.

I have been the longer on this argument, to prevent the reader's carrying what I ſay of the ſuperiority of *plays of character* to *plays of intrigue* into an extreme; a miſtake, into which ſome good writers have been unſuſpectingly betrayed by the acknowledged truth of the general principle. It is ſo natural for men, on all occaſions, to fly out into extremes, that too much care cannot be had to retain them in a due medium. But to return from this digreſſion to

the

the consideration of the difference of the two dramas.

3. A sameness of *character is not usually objected to in tragedy: in comedy, it would not be endured.* The passion of *avarice*, to resume the instance given above, being the main object, we find nothing but a disgustful repetition in a second attempt to delineate that *character*. *A particular cruel man* only engrossing our regard in *Nero*, when the train of events evidencing such cruelty is changed, we have all the novelty we look for, and can contemplate with pleasure the very *same* character, set forth by a different course of action, or displayed in some other *person*.

4. Comedy succeeds best when the scene is laid *at home*, tragedy for the most part when *abroad*. " This appears at first " sight whimsical and capricious, but has " its foundation in nature. What we chief- " ly seek in comedy is a true image of life " and *manners*; but we are not easily " brought to think we have it given us, " when dressed in foreign modes and fash- " ions. And yet a good writer must fol-

" low

"low his ſcene, and obſerve decorum. On "the contrary, it is the action in tragedy "which moſt engages our attention. But "to fit a domeſtic occurrence for the ſtage, "we muſt take greater liberties with the "action than a well-known ſtory will al-"low." [*Pope's Works*, vol. iv. p. 185.]

Other *characters* of the two dramas, as well *peculiar*, as *common*, which might be accounted for from the juſt notion of them, delivered above, I leave to the obſervation of the reader. For my intention is not to write a complete treatiſe on the drama, but briefly to lay down ſuch principles, from whence its *laws* may be derived.

CHAP. II.

OF THE GENIUS OF COMEDY.

BUT it may not be amiſs to expreſs myſelf a little more fully as to the *genius* of comedy; which, for want of paſſing through the hands of ſuch a critic, as Ariſtotle has been leſs perfectly underſtood.

Its *end* is the production of *humour*: or, which comes to the ſame thing, "of that "*pleaſure*,

" *pleasure*, which the *truth* of representa-
" tion affords, in the *exhibition* of the *pri-*
" *vate characters* of life, more particularly
" their *specific differences*." I add this *latter* clause, because the principal pleasure we take in contemplating characters consists in noting those *differences*. The general attributes of humanity, if represented ever so truly, give us but a slender entertainment. They, of course, make a part of the drama; but we chiefly delight in a picture of those peculiar *traits*, which distinguish the species. Now these discriminating marks in the characters of men are not *necessarily* the causes of ridicule, or pleasantry of any kind; but *accidentally*, and according to the nature or quality of them. The vanity, and impertinent boasting of *Thraso* is the natural object of *contempt*, and, when truly and forcibly expressed in his own character, provokes *ridicule*. The easy humanity of *Mitio*, which is the leading part of his character, is the object of *approbation*; and, when shewn in his own conduct, excites a *pleasure*, in common with all just *expression of the manners*,

 but

but of a *ſerious* nature, as being joined with the ſentiment of *eſteem.*

But now as moſt men find a greater pleaſure in gratifying the paſſion of *contempt*, than the calm inſtinct of *approbation*, and ſince perhaps the conſtitution of human life is ſuch, as affords more exerciſe for the one than the other, hence it hath come to paſs, that the comic poet, who paints for the generality, and follows nature, chuſes more commonly to ſelect and deſcribe thoſe *peculiarities* in the human character, which, by their nature, excite *pleaſantry*, than ſuch as create a ſerious regard and eſteem. Hence ſome perſons have appropriated the name of *comedies* to thoſe dramas, which chiefly aim at producing *humour*, in the more *proper* ſenſe of the word; under which view it means "ſuch an expreſſion or picture of what is "odd, or inordinate in each character, as "gives us the fulleſt and ſtrongeſt image "of the original, and by the truth of the "repreſentation expoſes the *ridicule* of it." And it is certain, that comedy receives great advantage from repreſentations of this

this kind. Nay, it cannot well ſubſiſt without them. Yet it doth not exclude the other and more *ſerious* entertainment, which, as it ſtands on the ſame foundation of *truth of repreſentation*, I venture to include under the *common term*.

Further, there are *two ways* of evidencing the characteriſtic and predominant qualities of men, or, of producing *humour*, which require to be obſerved. The *one* is, when they are ſhewn in the perpetual courſe and tenor of the repreſentation; that is, when the *humour* reſults from the *general* conduct of the perſon in the drama. and the diſcourſe, which he holds in it. The *other* is, when, by an happy and lively ſtroke, the characteriſtic quality is laid open and expoſed *at once*.

The *firſt* ſort of *humour* is that which we find in the antients, and eſpecially Terence. The *latter* is almoſt peculiar to the moderns; who, in uniting theſe two ſpecies of *humour*, have brought a vaſt improvement to the comic ſcene. The reaſon of this difference may perhaps have been the ſingular ſimplicity of the old writers, who were contented to take up with ſuch ſentiments or circumſtances, as moſt naturally and readily occurred in the courſe of the drama: whereas the moderns have been ambitious to ſhew a more exquiſite and ſtudied inveſtigation into the workings of human nature, and have ſought out for thoſe peculiarly ſtriking lineaments, in which the eſſence of character conſiſts. On the ſame account, I ſuppoſe, it was that the antients had *fewer* characters in their plays, than the moderns, and thoſe more *general*; that is, their dramatic writers were well ſatisfied with picturing the moſt *uſual* perſonages, and in their moſt *obvious* lights. They did not, as the moderns (who, if they would aſpire to the praiſe of *novelty*, were obliged to this route), caſt about for leſs *familiar* characters; and the nicer and *leſs obſerved* peculiarities which diſtinguiſh *each*. Be it as it will, the obſervation is certain. Later dramatiſts have apparently ſhewn a more accurate knowledge of human life: and, by opening theſe new and untryed veins of *humour*, have exceedingly enriched the comedy of our times.

But,

But, though we are not to look for the *two species of humour*, before-mentioned, in the same perfection on the simpler stages of *Greece and Rome*, as in *our* improved Theatres, yet the *first* of them was clearly seen and successfully practised by the antient comic masters; and there are not wanting in them some few examples even of the *last*. " The old man in the *Mother-*
" *in-Law* says to his Son,

Tum tu igitur nihil adtulisti huc plus unâ sententiâ.

" This, as an excellent person observed to
" me, is true *humour*. For his character,
" which was that of a lover of money,
" drew the observation naturally and forci-
" bly from him. His disappointment of a
" rich succession made him speak contempti-
" bly of a moral lesson, which rich and
" covetous men, in their best humours, have
" no high reverence for. And this too
" without *design*; which is important, and
" shews the distinction of what, in the more
" restrained sense of the word, we call *hu-*
" *mour*, from other modes of *pleasantry*.
" For had a young friend of the son, an un-
" concerned spectator of the scene, made

" the obſervation, it had then, in another's " mouth, been *wit*, or a deſigned *banter* on " the father's diſappointment. As, on the " other hand, when ſuch characteriſtic qua- " lities are exaggerated, and the expreſſion " of them ſtretched beyond *truth*, they be- " come *buffoonry*, even in the perſon's *own*."

This is an inſtance of the *ſecond ſpecies* of humour, under its idea of exciting *ridicule*. But it may, alſo, be employed with the utmoſt *ſeriouſneſs*; as being only a method of expreſſing the *truth* of character in the *moſt ſtriking* manner. This ſame *old man* in the Hecyra will furniſh an example. Though a lover of money, he appears, in the main, of an honeſt and worthy nature, and to have born the trueſt affection to an amiable and favourite ſon. In the perplexity of the ſcene, which had ariſen from the ſuppoſed miſunderſtanding between his *ſon's* wife and his *own*, he propoſes, as an expedient to end all differences, to retire with his wife into the country. And to enforce this propoſal to the young man, who had his reaſons for being againſt it, he adds,

od:oſa

odiosa haec est aetas adolescentulis:
E medio aequum excedere est: postremò nos jam fabula
Sumus, Pamphile, senex atque anus.

There is nothing, I ſuppoſe, in theſe words, which provokes a ſmile. Yet the *humour* is ſtrong, as before. In his ſolicitude to promote his ſon's ſatisfaction, he lets fall a ſentiment truly characteriſtic, and which old men uſually take great pains to conceal; I mean, his acknowledgment of *that ſuſpicious fear of contempt, which is natural to old age*. So true a picture of life, in the repreſentation of this *weakneſs*, might, in other circumſtances, have created ſome *pleaſantry*; but the *occaſion*, which forced it from him, diſcovering, at the ſame time, the *amiable diſpoſition* of the ſpeaker, covers the ridicule of it, or more properly converts it into an object of our *eſteem*.

We have here, then, a kind of *intermediate* ſpecies of *humour* betwixt the *ridiculous* and the *grave*; and may perceive how inſenſibly the *one* becomes the *other*, by the accidental mixture of a virtuous *quality*, attracting *eſteem*. Which may ſerve to reconcile the reader to the application of this *term* even to ſuch *expreſſion* of the manners, as is perfectly *ſerious*; that is, where the *quality repreſented* is entirely, and without the leaſt *touch* of attending ridicule, the object of *moral approbation* to the mind. As in that famous aſſeveration of Chremes in the *Self-tormentor*:

Homo ſum: humani nihil à me alienum puto.

This is a ſtrong expreſſion of character; and, coming unaffectedly from him in anſwer to the cutting reproof of his friend,

Chreme, tantumne ab re tuâ 'ſt oti tibi
Aliena ut cures; ea quae nihil ad te adtinent?

hath the eſſence of true *humour*, that is, is a *lively picture of the manners without deſign*.

Yet in this inſtance, which hath not been obſerved, the *humour*, though of a ſerious caſt, is heightened by a mixture of *ſatire*. For we are not to take this, as hath conſtantly been done, for a ſentiment of pure humanity and the natural ebullition of benevolence. We may obſerve in it a deſigned ſtroke of ſatirical reſentment.

The Self-tormentor, as we saw, had ridiculed Chremes' *curiosity* by a severe reproof. Chremes, to be even with him, reflects upon the *inhumanity* of his temper. "You," says he, "seem such a foe to humanity, "that you spare it not *in yourself*; I, on the "other hand, am affected, when I see it "suffer in *another*."

Whence we learn, that, though all which is requisite to constitute comic humour, be *a just expression of character without design*, yet such *expression* is felt more *sensibly*, when it is further enlivened by *ridicule*, or quickened by the poignancy of *satire*.

From the account of comedy, here given, it may appear, that the idea of this drama is much enlarged beyond what it was in Aristotle's time; who defines it to be, *an imitation of light and trivial actions, provoking ridicule*. His notion was taken from the state and practice of the Athenian stage; that is, from the *old* or *middle* comedy, which answers to this description. The great revolution, which the introduction of the *new comedy* made in the drama, did not happen till afterwards. This

proposed

proposed for its *object*, in general; *the actions and characters of ordinary life*; which are not, of necessity, ridiculous, but, as appears to every observer, of a mixt kind, *serious*, as well as *ludicrous*, and, within their proper sphere of influence, not unfrequently, even *important*. This kind of *imitation*, therefore, now admits the *serious*; and its scenes, even without the least mixture of *pleasantry*, are entirely *comic*. Though the common run of *laughers* in our theatre are so little aware of the extension of this *province*, that I should scarcely have hazarded the observation, but for the authority of *Terence*; who hath confessedly very little of the *pleasant* in his drama. Nay, one of the most admired of his comedies hath the gravity, and, in some places, almost the solemnity of *tragedy itself*. But this *idea* of comedy is not peculiar to the more polite and liberal *antients*. Some of the best *modern* comedies are fashioned in agreement to it. And an instance or two, which I am going to produce from the stage of simple nature, may seem to shew it the plain suggestion of common sense.

"The Amautas (says the author of the "*Royal Commentaries of* PERU), who were "men of the best ingenuity amongst them, "invented COMEDIES and TRAGEDIES; "which, on their solemn festivals, they re-"presented before the King and the Lords "of his court. The plot or argument of "their *tragedies* was, to represent *their* "*military exploits, and the triumphs, victo-*"*ries, and heroic actions, of their renowned* "*men*. And the subject or design of their "*comedies* was, to demonstrate *the man-*"*ner of good husbandry in cultivating and* "*manuring their fields, and to shew the* "*management of domestic affairs, with other* "*familiar matters*. These plays, continues "he, were not made up of obscene and "dishonest farces, but such as were of "*serious entertainment, composed of grave* "*and acute sentences*, &c."

Two things are observable in this brief account of the Peruvian drama. *First*, that its *species* had respect to the very different *objects* of the *higher* or *lower* stations. For the *great and powerful* were occupied in *war:* and *agriculture* was the chief employment of *private and ordinary life.* And, in this diſtinction, theſe *Indian* perfectly agreed with the old Roman poets; whoſe PRAETEXTATA and TOGATA ſhew, that they had preciſely the ſame ideas of the drama. *Secondly*, we do not learn only, what difference there *was* betwixt their tragedy and comedy, but we are alſo told, what difference there was *not*. It was not, that one was *ſerious*, and the other *pleaſant*. For we find it expreſsly aſſerted of *both*, that they *were of grave and ſerious entertainment*.

And this laſt will explain a ſimilar obſervation on the Chineſe, *who*, as P. DE PREMERE acquaints us, *make no diſtinction betwixt tragedies and comedies*. That is, *no diſtinction*, but what the different *ſubjects* of each make neceſſary. They do not, as our European dramas, differ in this, that the *one* is intended to make us *weep*, and the other to make us *laugh*.

Theſe are full and preciſe teſtimonies. For I lay no ſtreſs on what the Hiſtorian of *Peru* tells us, *that there were no obſcenities*

ties in their comedy, nor on what an encomiast of *China* pretends, *that there is not so much as an obscene word in all their language* [g]: as being sensible, that though indeed these must needs be considerable abatements to the *humour* of their comic scenes, yet, their ingenuity might possibly find means to remedy these defects by the invention and dextrous application of the *double entendre*, which, on our stage, is found to supply the place of rank *obscenity*, and, indeed, to do its office of exciting *laughter* almost as well.

But, as I said, there is no occasion for this *argument*. We may venture, without the help of it, to join these authorities to *that* of Terence; which, together, enable us to conclude very fully, in opposition to

[g] P. ALVAREZ SEMEDO, speaking of their poetry, says, "Le plus grand advantage et la plus "grande utilité qu'en ont tiré les CHINOIS, est cette "grande modestie et retenuë incomparable, qui se "voit en leurs ecrits, *n'ayant pas même une lettre en* "*tous leurs livres, ni en toutes leurs ecritures, pour ex*-"*primer les parties honteuses de la nature.*" [HIST. UNIV. DE LA CHINE, p. 82. à LYON 1667. 4to.]

the

the general ſentiment, that *ridicule* is not of the *eſſence of comedy* [*b*].

But, becauſe the general practice of the *Greek and Roman theatres*, which ſtrongly countenance the other opinion, may ſtill be thought to outweigh this ſingle *Latin poet*, together with all the *eaſtern and weſtern barbarians*, that can be thrown into the balance, let me go one ſtep further, and, by explaining the riſe and occaſion of this *practice*, demonſtrate, that, in the preſent caſe, their authority is, in fact, of no moment.

The form of the Greek, from whence the Roman and our drama is taken, though generally *improved* by reflexion and juſt criticiſm, yet, like ſo many other great inventions, was, in its original, the *product* of pure chance. Each of its ſpecies had ſprung out of a *chorus-ſong*, which was afterwards incorporated into the legitimate drama, and found eſſential to its true form. But *reaſon*, which ſaw to eſtabliſh what was

[*b*] Le ridicule est ce qu'il y a de plus essentiel a la Comedie. [P. Rapin, Reflex. sur la poet. p. 154. Paris 1684.]

right

right in this fortuitous conformation of the drama, did not equally succeed in detecting and separating what was *wrong*. For the *occasion* of this chorus-song, in their religious festivities, was widely different: the business, *at one time*, being to express their gratitude, in celebrating the praises of their gods and heroes; at *another*, to indulge their mirth, in jesting and sporting among themselves. The character of their drama, which had its rise from hence [*i*], conformed exactly to the difference of these *occasions*. *Tragedy*, through all its

[*i*] Οἱ μὲν σεμνότεροι τὰς καλὰς ἐμιμοῦντο πράξεις, καὶ τὰς τῶν τοιούτων τύχας· οἱ δὲ εὐτελέστεροι, τὰς τῶν φαύλων, ΠΡΩΤΟΝ ΨΟΓΟΥΣ ΠΟΙΟΥΝΤΕΣ, ΩΣΠΕΡ ΕΤΕΡΟΙ ΥΜΝΟΥΣ ΚΑΙ ΕΓΚΩΜΙΑ. [ΠΕΡ. ΠΟΙΗΤ. κδ.] This is Aristotle's account of the origin of the different *species of* POETRY. They were occasioned, he says, by the different and even opposite *tempers and dispositions of men: those of a loftier spirit delighting in the encomiastic poetry, while the humbler sort betook themselves to satire.* But this, also, is the just account of the rise and character of the different *species of the* DRAMA. For they grew up, he tells us in this very chapter, from the DITHYRAMBIC, and PHALLIC songs. And who were the *men*, who chaunted *these* but the ΣΕΜΝΟΤΕΡΟΙ, and ΕΥΤΕΛΕΣΤΕΡΟΙ, beforementioned? And how were they *employed* in them,

several

ſeveral ſucceſſive ſtages of improvement, was ſerious and even ſolemn. And a gay or rather buffoon ſpirit was the characteriſtic of *comedy*.

We ſee, then, the *genius* of theſe two poems was accidentally fixed in agreement to their reſpective *originals*; conſequent writers contenting themſelves to embelliſh and perfect, not *change*, the primary form. The practice of the antient ſtage is then of no further authority, than as it accords to juſt criticiſm. The ſolemn caſt of their *tragedy*, indeed, bears the teſt, and is found to be ſuitable to its real nature. The ſame does not appear of the burleſque form of *comedy*; no reaſon having been given, why *it* muſt, of neceſſity, have the *ridiculous* for its object. Nay, the effects of

but the *former, in hymning the praiſes of Bacchus; the latter, in dealing about obſcene jokes and taunting invectives on each other?* So that the *characters* of the men, and their *ſubjects*, being exactly the ſame in *both*, what is ſaid of the *one* is equally applicable to the *other*. It was proper to obſerve this; or the reader might, perhaps, object to the uſe made of this paſſage, *here*, as well as *above*, where it is brought to illuſtrate Ariſtotle's notion of the *natures* of the tragic and comic poetry.

improved

improved criticiſm on the later Greek comedy give a preſumption of the direct contrary. For, in proportion to the gradual refinement of this *ſpecies* in the hands of its greateſt maſters, the buffoon caſt of the comic drama was inſenſibly dropt, and even grew into a ſeverity, which departed at length very widely from the original idea. The admirable ſcholar of THEOPHRASTUS, who had been tutored in the exact ſtudy of human life, ſaw ſo much of the genuine character of true comedy, that he cleanſed it, at once, from the greater part of thoſe buffoonries, which had, till his time, defiled its nature. His great imitator, Terence, went ſtill further; and, whether impelled by his native humour, or determined by his truer taſte, mixed ſo little of the *ridiculous* in his comedy, as plainly ſhews, it might, in his opinion, ſubſiſt entirely without it. His *practice* indeed, and the theory, here delivered, nearly meet. And the concluſion is, that *comedy*, which is the image of private life, may take either character of *pleaſant* or *ſerious*, as it chances, or even *unite* them into one piece;

but that the *former* is by no means more eſſential to its conſtitution, than the *latter*.

I foreſee but one objection, that can be made to this theory; which has, in effect, been obviated already. "It may be ſaid, "that, if this account of *comedy* be juſt, it "would follow, that it might, with equal "propriety, admit the graveſt and moſt "affecting events, which inferior life fur-"niſhes, as the lighteſt. Whereas it is "notorious, that diſtreſſes of a deep and "ſolemn nature, though faithfully copied "from the fortunes of private men, would "never be endured, under the name of "*comedy*, on the ſtage. Nay, ſuch repre-"ſentations would rather paſs, in the pub-"lic judgment, for legitimate *tragedies*; of "which kind, we have, indeed, ſome exam-"ples in our language."

Two things are miſtaken in this objection. *Firſt*, it ſuppoſes, that deep diſtreſſes of every kind are inconſiſtent with comedy; the contrary of which may be learnt from the SELF-TORMENTOR of Terence. *Next*, it inſinuates, that, if deep diſtreſſes of any kind may be admitted

into

into comedy, the *deepest* may. Which is equally erroneous. For, the *manners* being the proper object of comedy, the *distress* must not exceed a certain degree of *severity*, lest it draw off the mind from them, and confine it to the *action* only: as would be the case of *murder*, *adultery*, and other atrocious crimes, infesting *private*, as well as *public*, life, were they to be represented, in all their horrors, on the stage. And though some of these, as *adultery*, have been brought, of late, into the comic scene; yet it was not till it had lost the atrocity of its nature, and was made the subject of mirth and pleasantry to the fashionable world. But for this happy disposition of the times, comedy, as managed by some of our writers, had lost its nature, and become *tragic*. And, yet, considered as *tragic*, such representations of low life had been improper. . Because, where the intent is to *affect*, the subject is with more advantage taken from *high life*, all the circumstances being, there, more peculiarly adapted to answer that end.

The ſolution then of the difficulty is, in one word, this. All *diſtreſſes* are not *improper* in comedy; but ſuch only as attach the mind to the *fable*, in neglect of the *manners*, which are its chief object. On the other hand, all *diſtreſſes* are not *proper* in tragedy; but ſuch only as are of force to intereſt the mind in the *action*, preferably to the obſervation of the *manners*; which can only be done, or is done moſt effectually, when the *diſtreſsful event*, repreſented, is taken from *public life*. So that the *diſtreſſes*, ſpoken of, are equally unſuited to what the natures *both* of *comedy and tragedy*, reſpectively, demand.

CHAP. III.

OF M. DE FONTENELLE'S NOTION OF COMEDY.

NOTWITHSTANDING the pains I have taken, in the preceding chapters, to eſtabliſh my theory of the comic drama, I find myſelf obliged to ſupport it ſtill further againſt the authority of a very eminent modern critic. M. de Fontenelle hath juſt now publiſhed two volumes of plays,

among

among which are ſome comedies of a very ſingular character. They are not only in a high degree *pathetic*; but the ſcene of them is laid in *antiquity*; and great perſonages, ſuch as *Kings*, *Princeſſes*, &c. are of the drama. He hath beſides endeavoured to juſtify this extraordinary ſpecies of comedy by a very ingenious preface. It will therefore be neceſſary for me to examine this new ſyſtem, and to obviate, as far as I can, the prejudices which the name of the author, and the intrinſic merit of the plays themſelves, will occaſion in favour of it.

His ſyſtem, as explained in the preface to theſe comedies, is, briefly, this.

" The *ſubject* of dramatic repreſenta-
" tion, he obſerves, is ſome event or action
" of *human life*, which can be conſidered
" only in two views, as being either that
" of *public*, or of *private*, perſons. The
" *end* of ſuch repreſentation, continues he,
" is to *pleaſe*, which it doth, either by
" engaging the attention, or by moving
" the paſſions. The *former* is done by
" repreſenting to us ſuch events as are

" *great, noble, or unexpected:* The *latter* by " ſuch as are *dreadful, pitiable, tender, or* " *pleaſant*. Of theſe ſeveral ſources of " *pleaſure*, he forms what he calls a *dramatic* " *ſcale*, the extremes of which he admits to " be altogether inconſiſtent; no art being " ſufficient to bring together the *grand*, the " *noble*, or the *terrible*, into the ſame piece " with the *pleaſant or ridiculous*. The im- " preſſions of theſe objects, he allows, are " perfectly oppoſed to each other. So " that a tragedy, which takes for its ſubject " a *noble*, or *terrible* event, can by no " means admit the *pleaſant*. And a co- " medy, which repreſents a *pleaſant* action, " can never admit the *terrible* or *noble*. " But it is otherwiſe, he conceives, with the " intermediate ſpecies of this ſcale. The " *ſingular*, the *pitiable*, the *tender*, which " fill up the interval betwixt the *noble* and " *ridiculous*, are equally conſiſtent with " tragedy and comedy. An uncommon " ſtroke of Fortune may as well befall a " peaſant as a prince. And two lovers of " an inferior condition may have as lively " a paſſion for each other, and, when ſome

" unlucky

" unlucky event separates them, may de-
" serve our pity as much, as those of the
" highest fortune. These situations then
" are equally suited to both dramas. They
" will only be modified in each a little differ-
" ently. From hence he concludes, that
" there may be *dramatic representations*,
" which are neither perfectly tragedies nor
" perfectly comedies, but yet partake of the
" nature of each, and that in different pro-
" portions. There might be a species of
" *tragedy*, for instance, which should unite
" the *tender* with the *noble* in any degree,
" or even subsist entirely by means of the
" *tender*: And of *comedy*, which should
" associate the *tender* with the *pleasant*, or
" even retain the *tender* throughout to a
" certain degree to the entire exclusion of
" the *pleasant*.

" As to his laying the *scene* of his co-
" medy in Greece, he thinks this practice
" sufficiently justified by the practice of the
" French writers, who make no scruple to
" lay their scene abroad, as in *Spain* or
" *England*.

" Laſtly, for what concerns the intro-" duction of great perſonages into the co-" mic drama, he obſerves, that by *ordinary* " *life*, which he ſuppoſes the proper ſub-" ject of comedy, he underſtands as well " that of Emperors and Princes, at times " when they are only men, as of inferior " perſons. And he thinks it very evident " that what paſſes in the ordinary *life*, ſo " underſtood, of the greateſt men, is truly " comick [*k*]."

This is a ſimple expoſition of M. de Fontenelle's idea of comedy, which, however, he hath ſet off with great elegance and a plauſibility of illuſtration, ſuch as writers of his claſs are never at a loſs to give to any ſubject they would recommend.

Now though the principal aim of what I have to offer in confutation of this ſyſtem be to combat the ingenious writer's notion of comedy; yet as the tenor of his *preface* leads him to deliver his ſentiments alſo of tragedy, I ſhall not ſcruple intermixing, after his example, ſome reflexions on this latter drama.

[*k*] *Pref. generale*, tom. vii. Par. 1751.

M. de

M. de Fontenelle ſets out with obſerving, that the end of dramatic repreſentation is to *pleaſe*. This end is very general. But he explains himſelf more preciſely, by ſaying, "*this pleaſure is of two kinds, and conſiſts either in attaching the mind, or affecting it.*" And this is not much amiſs. But his further explanation of theſe terms is ſuſpicious. "The mind, ſays he, is ATTACHED by the repreſentation of what is *great*, *noble*, *ſingular*, or *unexpected*: It is AFFECTED by what is *terrible*, *pitiable*, *tender*, or *pleaſant* [*l*]." In this enumeration, he forgets the merely *natural* draught of the manners. Yet this is ſurely one of the means by which the drama is enabled to *attach* the ſpectator. With me, I confeſs, this is the firſt excellence of comedy. Nor could he mean to include this ſource of pleaſure under his *ſecond* diviſion. For though a lively picture of the manners may in ſome ſort be ſaid to *affect* us, yet

[*l*] "On attache par le grand, par le noble, par le rare, par l'imprévû. On émeut par le terrible ou affreux, par le pitoyable, par le tendre, par le plaiſant ou ridicule." p. xiv.

certainly

certainly not as coming under the consideration of what is *terrible*, *pitiable*, *tender*, or *ridiculous*, but simply of what is *natural*. The picture is *pleasant* or otherwise, as it chances; but is always the source of entertainment to the observer. When the pleasantry is high, it takes indeed the passion of *ridicule*. In other instances, it can scarcely be said to *move*, " emouvoir." Now this I take to be a very considerable omission. For if the observation of character be a *pleasure*, which comedy is more particularly qualified to give, and which is not in any degree so compatible with tragedy, does not this bid fair for being the *proper* end of comedy? Human life, he says, which is the subject of the drama, can only be regarded in two views, as either that *of the great, and principally of kings*, and that of *private men*. Now the *attachments* and *emotions*, he speaks of, are excited more powerfully and to more advantage in a representation of the *former*. That which is *peculiar* to a draught of *ordinary life*, or which is attained *most perfectly* by it, is the delight arising from a just exhibition of the manners. No, he he will say. The *pleasant* belongs as peculiarly to a picture of common life, as the *natural*. Surely not. Common life *distorted*, or what we call *farce*, gives the entertainment of *ridicule* more perfectly than comedy. The only pleasure, which an exposition of *ordinary life* affords, distinct from that we receive from a view of *high life* on the one hand, and ordinary life *disfigured* on the other, is the satisfaction of contemplating the *truth of character*. However then this species of representation may be improved by incorporating other kinds of excellence with it, is not *this*, *of pleasing* by the *truth* of character, to be considered as the *appropriate* end of comedy?

I do not dispute the propriety of serious or even affecting comedies. I have already explained myself as to this point, and have shewn under what restrictions *the weeping comedy*, *la larmoyante comedie*, as the French call it, may be admitted on my plan. The main question is, whether there be any foundation in nature for two distinct and separate species *only* of the drama; or whether,

whether, as he pretends, a certain *ſcale*, which connects by an inſenſible communication the ſeveral modifications of dramatic repreſentation, unites and incorporates the two ſpecies into one.

It is true the laws of the drama, as formed by Ariſtotle out of the Greek poets, can of themſelves be no rule to us in this matter; becauſe theſe poets had given no example of ſuch intermediate ſpecies. This, for aught appears to the contrary, may be an extenſion of the province of the drama. The queſtion then muſt be tried by the ſucceſs of this new practice, compared with the general dictates of common ſenſe.

For I perfectly agree with this judicious critic, that we have a right to inquire if, in what concerns the ſtage, we are not ſometimes governed by *eſtabliſhed cuſtoms* inſtead of rules; for *rules* they will not deſerve to be eſteemed, till they have undergone the rigid ſcrutiny of reaſon [*m*].

[*m*] " Que nous ſommes en droit d'examiner ſi, " en fait de Theatre, nous n'aurions pas quelquefois " des *habitudes* au lieu de *regles*, car les regles ne

In respect of the *Practice*, then, it must be owned, there are many stories in private life capable of being worked up in such a manner as to move the passions strongly; and, on the contrary, many subjects taken from the great world capable of diverting the spectator by a pleasant picture of the manners. And lastly, it is also true, that both these ends may be affected together, in some degree, in either piece. But here is the point of enquiry. Whether, if the end in view be to *affect*, this will not be accomplished BETTER by taking a subject from the public than private fortunes of men: Or, if the end be to *please by the truth of character*, whether we are not likely to perceive this pleasure more FULLY when the story is of private, rather than of public life? For, as Aristotle said finely on a like occasion, *we are not to look for every sort of pleasure from tragedy* [or comedy], *but that which is peculiarly proper to each* [x].

" peuvent l'être qu'après avoir subi les rigueurs du
" tribunal de la raison." p. 37.

[x] Οὐ πᾶσαν δεῖ ζητεῖν ἡδονὴν ἀπὸ τραγῳδίας, ἀλλὰ τὴν οἰκείαν. Ποιητ. κ. ιδ'.

" Human

"Human life, this writer ſays, can be con-"ſidered but as *high* or *low*;" and "a re-"preſentation of it can pleaſe only as it "*attaches*, or *affects*." I aſk then, to which ſort of life ſhall the dramatic poet confine himſelf, when he would endeavour to raiſe theſe *affections* or theſe *attachments* to the higheſt pitch. The anſwer is plain. For if the poet would excite the tender paſſions, they will riſe higher of neceſſity, when awakened by noble ſubjects, than if called forth by ſuch as are of ordinary and familiar notice. This is occaſioned by what one may call a TRANSITION OF THE PASSIONS: that affection of the mind which is produced by the impreſſion of great objects, being more eaſily convertible into the ſtronger degrees of pity and commiſeration, than ſuch as ariſes from a view of the concerns of common life. The more *important* the intereſt, the greater part our minds take in it, and the more ſuſceptible are we of *paſſion*.

On the other hand, when the intended pleaſure is to reſult from ſtrong pictures of human nature, this will be felt more en-

tirely,

entirely, and with more sincerity, when we are at leisure to attend to them in the representation of inferior persons, than when the rank of the speaker, or dignity of the subject, is constantly drawing some part of our observation to itself. In a word, though *mixed dramas* may give us pleasure, yet the pleasure, in either kind, will be LESS in proportion to the mixture. And the *end* of each will be then attained MOST PERFECTLY when its character, according to the antient practice, is observed.

To consider then the writer's favourite position, that *le pitoyable* and *le tendre* are "common both to tragedy and comedy." The position, in general, is true. The difficulty is in fixing the degree, with which it ought to prevail in each. If *passion* predominates in a picture of private life, I call it a *tragedy* of private story, because it produces the *end* which tragedy designs. If *humour* predominates in a draught of public life, I call it a *comedy* of public story, because it gives the *pleasure* of pure comedy. Let these then be two new species of the drama, if you please, and let new

names

names be invented for them. Yet, were I a poet, I ſhould certainly adhere to the old practice. That is, if I wanted to produce *paſſion*, I ſhould think myſelf able to raiſe it higheſt on a great ſubject. And if I aimed to *attach* by *humour*, I ſhould depend on catching the whole attention of the ſpectator more ſucceſsfully on a familiar ſubject.

But by a *familiar ſubject*, this critic will ſay, he means, as I do, a ſubject taken from *ordinary life*; and that the affairs of kings and princes may very properly come into comedy under this view. Beſides the reaſon already produced againſt this innovation, I have this further exception to it. The buſineſs of comedy, he will allow, is in part at leaſt to exhibit the *manners*. Now the princely or heroic comedy is ſingularly improper for this end. If perſons of ſo diſtinguiſhed a rank be the actors in comedy, propriety demands that they be ſhewn in conformity to their characters in real life. But now that very politeneſs, which reigns in the courts of princes and the houſes of the great, prevents the *manners* from ſhew-

ing

ing themselves, at least with that distinctness and *relief* which we look for in dramatic characters. Inferior personages, acting with less reserve and caution, afford the fittest occasion to the poet of expressing their genuine tempers and dispositions. Or, if a picture of the manners be expected from the introduction of great persons, it can be only in tragedy, where the importance of the interests, and the strong play of the passions, strip them of their borrowed disguises, and lay open their true characters. So that the princely, or *heroic*, comedy, is the least fitted, of any kind of drama, to furnish this pleasure.

The antients appear to have had no doubt at all on the matter. The tragedy on low life, and comedy on high life, were refinements altogether unknown to them. What then hath occasioned this revolution of taste amongst us? Principally, I conceive, these three things.

1. The comedy on high life hath arisen from a *different state of government*. In the free towns of Greece there was no room for that distinction of high and low comedy,

which the moderns have introduced. And the reaſon was, the members of thoſe communities were ſo nearly on a level, that any one was a repreſentative of the reſt. There was no ſtanding ſubordination of royalty, nobility, and commonalty, as with us. Their way of ennobling their characters was by making them Generals, Ambaſſadors, Magiſtrates, &c. and then, in that public view, they were fit perſonages for tragedy. When ſtripped of theſe enſigns of authority, they became ſimple citizens.

Amongſt us, perſons of elevated rank make a ſeparate order in the community, whoſe private lives however might, no doubt, be the ſubject of comic repreſentation. Why then are not theſe fit perſonages for comedy? The reaſon has been given. They want *dramatic manners.* Or if they did not, their elevated and ſeparate eſtate makes the generality conceive with ſuch reverence of them, that it would ſhock their notions of high life to ſee them employed in a courſe of comic adventures. And of this M. de Fontenelle himſelf was ſufficiently ſenſible. For ſpeaking in another

other place of the importance which the tragic action receives from the dignity of its persons, he says, " When the actions are " of such a kind as that, without losing any " thing of their beauty, they might pass be- " tween inferior persons, the names of kings " and princes are nothing but a foreign " ornament which the poet gives to his " subject. Yet *this ornament, foreign as it " may be, is necessary: so fated are we to be " always dazzled by titles* [o]." Should he not have seen then, that this pageantry of titles, which is so requisite to raise the dignity of the tragic drama, must for the same reason prevent the familiarity of the comic? The great themselves are, no doubt, in this, as other instances, above *vulgar* prejudices. But the dramatic poet writes for the people.

2. The tragedy on low life, I suspect, has been chiefly owing to our *modern romances*: which have brought the tender passion into great repute. It is the constant and almost sole object of *le pitoyable* and *le tendre* in our drama. Now the prevalency

[o] *Reflex. sur la poës.* p. 232.

of this paſſion, in all degrees, hath made it thought an indifferent matter, whether the ſtory, that exemplifies it, be taken from low or high life. As it rages equally in both, the pathos, it was believed, would be juſt the ſame. And it is true, if tragedy confine itſelf to the diſplay of this paſſion, the difference will be leſs ſenſible than in other inſtances. Becauſe the concern terminates more directly in the *tender pair* themſelves, and does not ſo neceſſarily extend itſelf to others. Yet to heighten this ſame pathos by the *grand* and *important*, would methinks be the means of affording a ſtill higher pleaſure.

8. After all, that effuſion of *ſoftneſs* which prevails to ſuch a degree in all our dramas, comic as well as tragic, to the excluſion of every other intereſt, is, perhaps, beſt accounted for by this writer. As the matter is delicate, I chuſe to give it in his own words: " On s'imagine naturellement, " que les piéces Grecques & les nôtres ont " été jugées au même tribunal, à celui d'un " public aſſés egal dans les deux nations; " mais cela n'eſt pas tout-a-fait vrai. Dans

" le

" le tribunal d'Athenes, *les femmes* n'avoient " pas de voix, ou n'en avoient que trés " peu. Dans le tribunal de Paris, c'est " précisément le contraire; ici il est donc " question de plaire aux femmes, qui assuré- " ment aimeront mieux le pitoyable & le " tendre, que terrible et méme le grand." He adds, " *Et je ne crois pas au fond qu'elles " ayent grand tort.*" And what gallant man but would subscribe to this opinion?

On the whole, this attempt of M. de Fontenelle, to innovate in the province of comedy, puts one in mind of that he made, many years ago, in pastoral poetry. It is exactly the same spirit which has governed this polite writer in both adventures. He was once for bringing courtiers in masquerade into *Arcadia*. And now he would set them unmasked on the comic stage. Here, at least, he thought they would be in place. But the simplicity of pastoral dialogue would not suffer the one; and the familiarity of comic action forbids the other. It must be confessed, however, he hath succeeded better in the example of his comedies, than his pastorals. And no wonder.

For what we call the *fashions* and *manners* are confined to certain conditions of life, so that *pastoral courtiers* are an evident contradiction and absurdity. But the *appetites* and *passions* extending through all ranks, hence low tricks and low amours are thought to suit the minister and sharper alike. However it be, the fact is, that M. de Fontenelle hath succeeded best in his *comedies*. And as his theory is likely to gain more credit from the success of his practice than the force of his reasoning, I think it proper to close these remarks with an observation or two upon it.

There are, I observed, three things to be considered in his comedies, *his introduction of great personages, his practice of laying the scene in antiquity, and his pathos*.

Now to see the impropriety of the *first* of these innovations, we need only observe with what art he endeavours to conceal it. His very dexterity in managing his comic heroes clearly shews the natural repugnance he felt in his own mind betwixt the representation of such characters, and even his own idea of the comic drama.

The

The TYRANT is a ſtrange title of a comedy. It required ſingular addreſs to familiarize this frightful perſonage to our conceptions. Which yet he hath tolerably well done, but by ſuch expedients as confute his general theory. For to bring him down to the level of a comic character, he gives us to underſtand, that the *Tyrant* was an uſurper, who from a very mean birth had forced his way into the tyranny. And to lower him ſtill more, we find him repreſented, not only as odious to his people, but of a very contemptible character. He further makes him the tyrant only of a ſmall Greek town; ſo that he paſſes, with the modern reader, for little more than the Mayor of a corporation. There is alſo a plain illuſion in making a *ſimple citizen* demand his daughter in marriage. For under the cover of this word, which conveys the idea of a perſon in lower life, we think very little of the dignity of a free citizen of Corinth. Whence it appears that the poet felt the neceſſity of unkinging this tyrant as far as poſſible, before he could make a comic character of him.

The caſe of his ABDOLONIME is ſtill eaſier. It is true, the ſtructure of the fable requires us to have an eye to royalty; but all the pride and pomp of the regal character is ſtudiouſly kept out of ſight. Beſides, the affair of royalty does not commence till the action draws to a concluſion, the perſons of the drama being all ſimple particulars, and even of the loweſt figure, through the entire courſe of it.

The King of Sidon is, further, a paltry ſovereign, and a creature of Alexander. And the characters of the perſons, which are indeed admirably touched, are purpoſely contrived to leſſen our ideas of ſovereignty.

The LYSIANASSE is a tragedy in form, of that kind which hath a happy cataſtrophe. The *perſons*, *ſubject*, every thing ſo important, and attaches the mind ſo intirely to the event, that nothing intereſts more.

As to his *laying the ſcene in antiquity, and eſpecially in the free towns of Greece*, I would recommend it as an admirable expedient to all thoſe who are diſpoſed to follow

follow him in this new province of heroic comedy. For amongst other advantages, it gives the writer an occasion to fill the courts of his princes with *simple citizens*, which, as was observed, by no means answer to our ideas of nobility. But in any other view I cannot say much for the practice. It is for obvious reasons highly inconvenient. Even this writer found it so, when in one of his plays, the MACATE, he was obliged to break through the propriety of antient manners in order to adapt himself to the modern taste. His duel, as he himself says, "*a l'air bien François et* "*bien peu Grec.*" The reader, if he pleases, may see his apology for this transgression of decorum. Or, if there were no inconvenience of this sort, the representation of characters after the *antique* must, on many occasions, be cold and disgusting. At least none but professed scholars can be taken with it.

Nor is the usage of the Latin writers any precedent. For, besides that Horace, we know, condemned it as suitable only to the infancy of their comic poetry, the manners,

ners, laws, reilgion of the Greeks were in the main ſo ſimilar to their own, that the difference was hardly diſcernible. Or if it were otherwiſe in ſome points, the neighbourhood of this famous people and the intercourſe the Romans had with them, would bring them perfectly acquainted with ſuch difference. And this laſt reflexion ſhews how inſufficient it was for the author to excuſe his own practice from the authority of his countrymen; who, ſays he, "never ſcruple laying their ſcene in "Spain or England." Are the manners of antient Greece as familiar to a French pit, as thoſe of theſe two countries?

Laſtly, I have very little to object to the *pathos* of his comedy. When it is ſubſervient to the *manners*, as in the TESTAMENT and ABDOLONIME, I think it admirable. When it exceeds this degree, and takes the attention intirely, as in the LYSIANASSE, it gives a pleaſure indeed, but not the pleaſure appropriate to comedy. I regard it as a faint imperfect ſpecies of tragedy. After all, I fear, the *tender and pitiable* in comedy, though it

muſt

muſt afford the higheſt pleaſure to ſenſible and elegant minds, is not perfectly ſuited to the apprehenſions of the generality. Are they ſuſceptible of the ſoft and delicate emotions which the fine diſtreſs in the *Teſtament* is intended to raiſe? Every one indeed is capable of being delighted through the *paſſions*; but they muſt be worked up, as in tragedy, to a greater height, before the generality can receive that delight from them. The ſame objection, it will be ſaid, holds againſt the finer ſtrokes of character. Not, I think, with the ſame force. I doubt our ſenſe of imitation, eſpecially of the *ridiculous*, is quicker than our humanity. But I determine nothing. Both theſe pleaſures are perfectly conſiſtent. And my idea of comedy requires only that the *pathos* be kept in ſubordination to the *manners*.

CHAP.

CHAP. IV.

OF THE PROVINCE OF FARCE.

THUS much then for the general idea of COMEDY. If confidered more accurately it is, further, of *two kinds*. And in confidering thefe we fhall come at a juft notion of the province of FARCE. For this *mirror of private life* either, 1. reflects fuch qualities and characters, as are common *to human nature at large*: or, 2. it reprefents the whims, extravagances, and caprices, which characterize the folly of *particular perfons or times*.

Again, *each* of thefe is, further, to be fubdivided into *two fpecies*. For 1. the reprefentations of *common nature* may either be taken *accurately*, fo as to reflect *a faithful and exact image* of their original; which alone is *that* I would call COMEDY, as beft agreeing to the defcription which Cicero gives of it, when he terms it IMAGINEM VERITATIS. Or, they may be forced and overcharged above the fimple and juft proportions of *nature*; as when the

the excesses of a *few* are given for *standing* characters, when not the man is described, but the *passion*, or when, in the draught of the man, the leading *feature* is extended beyond measure: And in these cases the representation holds of the lower province of FARCE. In like manner, 2. the other *species*, consisting in the representation of *partial nature*, either transcribes such characters as are peculiar to *certain countries or times*, of which *our comedy* is, in great measure, made up; or it presents the image of *some real individual person*; which was the distinguishing character of the *old comedy* properly so called.

Both these kinds evidently belong to FARCE: not only as failing in that general and universal imitation of nature, which is alone deserving the name of comedy, but, also, for this reason, that, being more directly written for the present purpose of discrediting certain *characters* or *persons*, it is found convenient to exaggerate their peculiarities and enlarge their features;

and

and ſo, on a double account, they are to be referred to that *claſs*.

And thus the *three forms of dramatic compoſition*, the only ones which good ſenſe acknowledges, are kept diſtinct: and the proper END and CHARACTER of each, clearly underſtood.

1. *Tragedy and Comedy*, by their lively but faithful repreſentations, cannot fail to *inſtruct*. Such natural exhibitions of the human character, being ſet before us in the clear mirror of the drama, muſt needs ſerve to the higheſt *moral uſes*, in awakening that inſtinctive approbation, which we cannot withhold from *virtue*, or in provoking the not leſs neceſſary deteſtation of *vice*. But this, though it be their beſt *uſe*, is by no means their primary *intention*. Their proper and immediate *end* is, to PLEASE: the *one*, more eſpecially by intereſting the *affections*; the *other*, by *a juſt and delicate imitation of real life*. *Farce*, on the contrary, profeſſes to *entertain*; but this, in order more effectually to

ſerve

ſerve the intereſts of virtue and good ſenſe. Its proper *end* and purpoſe (if we allow it to have any reaſonable one) is, then, to INSTRUCT. Which the reader will underſtand me as ſaying, not of what we know by the name of *farce* on the modern ſtage (whoſe *prime* intention can hardly be thought even that low one, aſcribed to it by Mr. Dryden, *of* entertaining *citizens, country gentlemen, and Covent-Garden fops)*, but of the legitimate *end* of this *drama*; known to the Antients under the name of the *old Comedy*, but having neither name nor exiſtence, properly ſpeaking, among the Moderns. Of which we may ſay, as Mr. Dryden did, but with leſs propriety, of Comedy, "*That it is a ſharp manner of* " inſtruction *for the vulgar, who are never* " *well amended, till they are more than ſuf-* " *ficiently expoſed.*" [Pref. to Tranſ. of Freſnoy, p. xix.]

2. Though tragedy and comedy reſpect the *ſame general* END, yet purſuing it by *different means*; hence it comes to paſs, their CHARACTERS are wholly different.

For

For tragedy, aiming at *pleaſure* principally through the *affections*, whoſe flow muſt not be checked and interrupted by any counter impreſſions: and comedy, as we have ſeen, addreſſing itſelf *principally* to our *natural ſenſe of reſemblance and imitation*; it follows, that the *ridiculous* can never be aſſociated with tragedy, without deſtroying its *nature*, though with the *ſerious comic* it very well conſiſts.

And here the *practice* coincides with the *rule*. All exact writers, though they conſtantly mix *grave and pleaſant* ſcenes together in the ſame *comedy*, yet never preſume to do this in *tragedy*, and ſo keep the two ſpecies of *tragedy and comedy* themſelves perfectly diſtinct. But,

3. It is quite otherwiſe with *comedy* and *farce*. Theſe almoſt perpetually run into each other. And yet the reaſon of the thing demands as intire and perfect a ſeparation in this caſe, as in the other. For the perfection of *comedy* lying in the accuracy and fidelity of univerſal repreſentation, and *farce* profeſſedly neglecting or rather purpoſely

posely transgressing the limits of common nature and just decorum, they clash entirely with each other. And *comedy* must so far fail of giving the *pleasure*, appropriate to its design, as it allies itself with *farce*; while *farce*, on the other hand, forfeits the *use*, it intends, of promoting popular ridicule, by restraining itself within the exact rules of *Nature* which Comedy observes.

But there is little occasion to guard against this *latter* abuse. The danger is all on the other side. And the passion for what is now called *Farce*, the shadow of the Old Comedy, has, in fact, possessed the modern poets to such a degree, that we have scarcely one example of a comedy without this gross mixture. If any are to be excepted from this censure in Moliere, they are his *Misanthrope*, and *Tartuffe*; which are accordingly, by common allowance, the best of his large collection. In proportion as his other plays have less or more of this farcical turn, their true value hath been long since determined.

Of our own comedies, such of them, I mean, as are worthy of criticism, Ben Jonſon's *Alchemiſt* and *Volpone* bid the faireſt for being written in this genuine unmixed manner. Yet, though their merits are very great, ſevere Criticiſm might find ſomething to object even to theſe. The ALCHEMIST, ſome will think, is exaggerated throughout; and ſo, at beſt, belongs to that ſpecies of comedy which we have before called *particular and partial.* At leaſt, the extravagant purſuit, ſo ſtrongly expoſed in that play, hath now, of a long time, been forgotten; ſo that we find it difficult to enter fully into the humour of this highly-wrought character. And, in general, we may remark of ſuch characters, that they are a ſtrong temptation to the writer to exceed the bounds of truth in his draught of them at *firſt*, and are further liable to an imperfect, and even unfair, ſentence from the reader *afterwards.* For the welcome reception, which theſe pictures of prevailing *local* folly meet with on the ſtage, cannot but induce the poet, almoſt without deſign, to inflame the repreſentation: and the want of *archetypes*, in a little time, makes it paſs for immoderate,

derate, were it originally given with ever ſo much diſcretion and juſtice. So that, whether the *Alchemiſt* be farcical or not, it will *appear*, at leaſt, to have this note of Farce, "That the principal character is "exaggerated." But then this is all we muſt affirm. For, as to the *ſubject* of this Play's being a *local folly*, which ſeems to bring it directly under the denomination of Farce, it is but juſt to make a diſtinction. Had the *end and purpoſe* of the Play been to expoſe *Alchemy*, it had been liable to this objection. But this mode of *local folly* is employed as the *means* only of expoſing *another* folly, extenſive as our Nature, and coeval with it, namely *Avarice*. So that the ſubject has all the requiſites of true *Comedy*. It is juſt otherwiſe, we may obſerve, in the *Devil's an Aſs*; which therefore properly falls under our cenſure. For there, the folly of the time, *Projects and Monopolies*, are brought in to be expoſed as the *end and purpoſe* of the comedy.

On the whole, the *Alchemiſt* is a Comedy in juſt form, but a little *Farcical* in the extenſion of one of its characters.

The VOLPONE is a ſubject ſo manifeſtly fitted for the entertainment of all times, that it ſtands in need of no vindication. Yet neither, I am afraid, is this Comedy, in all reſpects, a complete model. There are even ſome Incidents of a farcical invention; particularly, the *Mountebank Scene*, and *Sir Politique's Tortoiſe*, are in the taſte of the *old comedy*; and without its rational purpoſe. Beſides, the *humour* of the dialogue is ſometimes on the point of becoming inordinate, as may be ſeen in the pleaſantry of *Corbaccio's miſtakes through deafneſs*, and in other inſtances. And we ſhall not wonder, that the beſt of his plays are liable to ſome objections of this ſort, if we attend to the *character* of the writer. For his nature was ſevere and rigid; and this, in giving a ſtrength and manlineſs, gave at times too an intemperance to his ſatyr. His taſte for ridicule was ſtrong, but indelicate; which made him not over-curious in the choice of his *topics*. And, laſtly, his *ſtyle* in picturing characters, though maſterly, was without that elegance of *hand* which is required to correct and allay the force of of ſo bold a colouring. Thus, the biaſs of his nature leading him to Plautus, rather than Terence, for his model, it is not to be wondered, that his wit is too frequently cauſtic, his raillery coarſe, and his humour exceſſive.

Some later writers for the ſtage have, no doubt, avoided theſe defects of the exacteſt of our old dramatiſts. But do they reach his excellencies? Poſterity, I am afraid, will judge otherwiſe, whatever may be now thought of ſome more faſhionable comedies. And, if they do not, neither the ſtate of general manners, nor the turn of the public taſte, appears to be ſuch as countenances the expectation of greater improvements. To thoſe, who are not over-ſanguine in their hopes, our forefathers will perhaps be thought to have furniſhed (what in nature ſeem linked together) the faireſt example of *dramatic*, as of *real manners*.

But here it will probably be ſaid, an affected zeal for the honour of our old poets has betrayed their unwary advocate into a conceſſion which diſcredits his whole pains on this ſubject. For to what purpoſe, may it be aſked, this waſte of dramatic criticiſm, when, by the allowance of the idle ſpeculatiſt himſelf, his theory is likely to prove ſo unprofitable, at leaſt, if it be not ill-founded? The only part I can take in this nice conjuncture is, to ſcreen myſelf behind the authority of a much abler critical theoriſt, who had once the misfortune to find himſelf in theſe unlucky circumſtances, and has apologized for it. The *objection* is fairly urged by this fine writer; and, in ſo profound and ſpeculative an age as the preſent, I preſume to ſuggeſt no other anſwer than he has thought fit to give to it. "Speculations of this ſort, ſays he, do not "beſtow genius on thoſe who have it not; "they do not perhaps afford any great "aſſiſtance to thoſe who have; and moſt "commonly the men of genius are even "incapable of being aſſiſted by ſpeculation. "To what uſe then do they ſerve? why, "to lead up *to the firſt principles of beauty* "ſuch perſons as love reaſoning, and are "fond of reducing, under the controul of "philoſophy, ſubjects that appear the

" most independent of it, and which are
" generally thought abandoned to the ca-
" price of taste [p]."

[p] " Ces sortes de speculations ne donnent point " de genie à ceux qui en manquent; elles n'aident " beaucoup ceux qui en ont: et le plus souvent même " les gens de génie sont incapables d'être aidées par " les speculations. A quoi donc sont-elles bonnes? " A faire remonter jusqu'aux premieres idées du beau " quelques gens qui aiment la raisonnement, et se " plaisent à reduire sous l'empire de la philosophie " les choses qui en paroissent le plus indépendantes, " et que l'on croit communément abandonnées à la " bizarrerie des goûts." M. DE FONTENELLE.

The END *of the* SECOND VOLUME.

www.ingramcontent.com/pod-product-compliance
Lightning Source LLC
Chambersburg PA
CBHW020051030726
47498CB00006B/1732
9783337399306